D1620368

CROMBY'S AXIOM

GARY J. KIRCHNER

 FriesenPress

Suite 300 - 990 Fort St
Victoria, *BC, V8V 3K2*
Canada

www.friesenpress.com

This book is a work of fiction. Characters and incidents are products of the
author's imagination. Any resemblance to actual persons, places, or events is
coincidental. The name 'Antikagamac' comes from the name of a lake in Parc de la
Mauricie, Quebec.

Cover illustration by Tyra Schad

ISBN
978-1-5255-9608-7 (Hardcover)
978-1-5255-9607-0 (Paperback)
978-1-5255-9609-4 (eBook)

1. Fiction, Dystopian

Distributed to the trade by The Ingram Book Company

To David Lawrence,
who always had the courage to follow his heart,
the conviction to do what was right,
and the judgement to keep things in perspective.
Happy trails.

PART 1

Look: a mountain meadow sweeps softly downward in vertiginous splendour. It is dotted with millions of white and yellow flowers, daisies and dandelions and buttercups, brilliant in the golden afternoon sunshine. Look more closely: blue flowers – thistle and clover and columbines and delicate bluebells – undulate in the gentle breeze along with the wild waist-high grass. Bees drift from one flower to another, and the *TZSTST-TZSTST* and *CHIIIRP-CHIIIRP* sounds of grasshoppers and crickets come from everywhere. Overhead, three crows soar, black, and did you notice that there is a split, a minor injury, in the tail-feathers of the third one? A few puffy white clouds float unencumbered here and there in the azure sky, and larger ones in the distance cut off the peaks of granite-faced mountains.

A path traverses the meadow horizontally, bordered on its uphill side by a low fence that consists of nothing more than two strands of rusting barbed wire attached to decaying wooden posts. At the edge of the path, wild strawberries grow, tiny and red and succulent in their late-June ripeness. You can almost taste them, can't you? In the field, far above the fence, a half-dozen wild alpacas stand, gazing outward as if contemplating a question in mathematics. There was a time when cows would have grazed here, their cow-bells clanging like discordant church bells. But of course, that would have been decades ago.

Look: a man is running along the path. A big, huge man, six and a half feet tall if he's an inch, but he's not moving straight up as, say, someone out for a jog. No, he's crooked, bent over, at times almost touching the ground with his hands. In fact, his gaze is fixed on the ground a metre in front of his feet, as if he's afraid to look anywhere else. He seems to be in a great hurry, and he's panting and gasping and making the throttling noise of someone at the point of exhaustion.

Look more closely: he's sweating profusely, but it's a cold sweat. His face is ghastly white, almost waxy. His hair is dishevelled. His eyes are wild. His lips are pulled back so that you can see both the upper and the lower teeth. It is the face, one can only conclude, of either a madman or of one in the grip of absolute, sheer, utter terror.

*   *   *   *   *

1

Thomas Pierre Antikagamac stumbled because of encroaching exhaustion, almost tumbling down the steep slope. This, despite the fact his debilitating fear of heights had him leaning into the hillside and bent almost double, so that sometimes he skimmed the ground with his hands. A weak and pathetic sound escaped his lips, a kind of *AAaaaaa!* that would be more expected of a child than of a huge man with the chiselled physique of a professional athlete. The stumble made him pause for the first time since he'd panicked. The valley, unfathomably far below, tugged at him with seductive strength, and he sank to his hands and knees, grasping weeds with his fingers for security. He felt his arms shaking and was afraid they would lose their strength: he would be pulled over the edge and roll to his death. He was powerless to stop the tremors. His wide eyes refused to close; with an effort, he forced his head to turn so that his gaze was towards the inside of the path. He saw a strand of barbed wire, and he absently considered grabbing hold of it.

Breath came in rapid and shallow bursts, his constricted chest forcing him to pant noisily like a dog. A hysterical dog. And like a hysterical dog, he was compelled to keep moving. He didn't know why. He didn't know where he was; he didn't know where he was going. His brain was white noise. He began to crawl, tentatively at first, but then with a bit more authority as he gained confidence in the stability of his position with its low centre of gravity and its six points of ground contact. How humiliating it would be if anyone had been around to see him like this.

And that was the first clear thought that had coalesced in his head since he'd lost the connection to the Hive.

At the present moment, he couldn't care less about humiliation. He just wanted to get . . . somewhere. Out of here. Off this teetering slope. Yes. Somewhere. Please. Somewhere.

The connection was broken. He was an astronaut tumbling through space, cut off from his ship, his jets dead.

No. It will come back. It was just a glitch of some sort in the Mother. It was known to happen. And he had been taught – heck, every child was taught – what to do. What to do just in case something like this happens.

And, of course, what to do is *"Don't panic!"*

Well, that doesn't help very much, because you can't think about not panicking when you are utterly panicked.

Gradually, as he crawled, his cognitive powers returned. *The path was wider than a sidewalk,* he told himself. Was there any reason why he would fall off a sidewalk? If he was crawling on his hands and knees?

The difference was that a sidewalk was all of 8 inches above the street.

He glanced, without intending to, down the steep slope to his right. *Oh shit!* Oh *shitshitshitshit!* He froze in place, clasped his hands on the weeds more tightly, and clamped his eyes shut.

There'd been a movie on the wall-screen when he was a small child, and he'd already been afraid of heights. All he remembered of the movie was that there was a tall tower, and somebody had to go up to the top of the tower to see something, to scout the surroundings. Nobody wanted to go up, because at the top you were exposed, and whoever went up invariably got shot with an arrow – it must have been an old Western movie – and fell out. He didn't remember anything else, except the dread in his chest when someone was ordered to the top of the tower. When the movie was over, his father snatched him with his big hands and hoisted him overhead, shouting, "UP in the tower!" Thomas shrieked and shrieked in terror until his father, laughing, put him down, and then he was hoisted again. "UP in the tower!" He screamed and cried, his father having a great time, his mother saying, "Oh, for heaven's sake Paul, put him down. You're scaring him . . ." his feet barely touching the ground before, "UP in the tower! . . ."

He opened his eyes, forced himself to move on. That was, of course, before his connection, before he'd become part of the Hive. So he'd certainly been less than five.

He was pleading for that connection right now. *Come on! Come on!* He'd never known anyone who had had to suffer through a glitch, but he knew that they did happen. The Mother wasn't perfect, after all, although it was becoming more and more reliable. Glitches typically lasted for a few seconds; the longest he'd ever heard of had lasted a bit over an hour.

How long had *he* been out now? Hours? Could it have only been minutes?

When the connection had first broken, he'd screamed and screamed. Some primal instinct made him run, run wildly. A hysterical dog. There was no thought as to where; in fact, there was no thought at all. His head was empty except for static: empty of friends, *Agies, Map-pleaser, S'uP?,* the *BOK* . . . All he had was himself, a blind rubber ball propelled in an empty universe.

It would make anyone insane.

Okay, he was thinking again, to a certain degree anyway. Where was he? No idea. And without the connection, he had no way of knowing. He'd been running along a trail somewhere, off-season training, in Switzerland, in the Fallowlands. Then he lost his mind. Now he was here.

What were they all taught to do if there was a glitch? Besides not panic? Stop. Don't move. Sit comfortably, close your eyes, and just listen to the static. Don't think about anything except that the glitch will be fixed within a very short time. The connection will be re-established. All will be well. Just sit, listen to the static, and don't think about anything.

Up ahead, the grass of the slope gave way to trees. If he could make it there, he would feel secure. Surrounded by trees, the vertigo would be gone. Surrounded by trees, he wouldn't fall to his death so easily.

He crawled on. When he reached the forested area, the connection still had not been restored. But it was shady, and the trees gave him some relief from his acrophobia. Still, the slope down was frightening. Amazing that trees could grow on terrain that was so steep. *Stop bloody thinking!*

Since his connection when he was a child, the support of the Hive had all but eliminated his fear of heights, to the point that he'd practically forgotten about it.

What happened to the connection!

The barbed wire had ended at the trees, and he sat facing outward, his knees hugged to his chest, his lower back touching the uphill slope behind him. He was alone, totally alone with his thoughts. He felt at that moment like the loneliest person in the world, and the weight of the loneliness was crushing. He closed his eyes and tried to think of nothing. It was impossible.

An hour passed. Or was it 10 minutes? Or three hours? Without the connection, he had no way of knowing. The sun was moving further and further to his right; he must be facing south, and the time was late afternoon. Then the sun slid behind the mountain he was traversing, and the dimness in the shade deepened, becoming crepuscular. He could still see sunlight on the distant mountains, glimpsed in places through the trees. What time was sunset: 21:00? Panic began building in his throat, as it had several times; he swallowed consciously. Why was he still disconnected?

What if it never came back?

He shifted position, moved onto his knees. His buttocks were numb from the lack of circulation. In time, shadows crept up the far mountains, and nightfall came. Still, he was alone in his head, as alone and distinctly separate from his fellows as from each of these trees around him. With the evening, the mountain air became surprisingly cool, and now with nightfall, it was quite chill. But, at least as far as temperature was concerned, Tommy was quite comfortable. His training outfit was AckerWear. "Ultra-dry, Ultra-breathable, Ultra-cool in the heat, Ultra-warm in the cold. AckerWear Ultra: light and snug as a second skin," went the clothing tag. Expensive as emperor's piss, mind you, but money wasn't a concern. With his salary, Tommy Antikagamac could afford anything.

Fatigue began to overtake him. When it was quite dark, he finally lay down on the path, staring up at the slit of sky between the trees on either side. The sky was inky black, and stars he couldn't identify shone with surpassing brilliance, like holes poked through the celestial vault. So different from the vague, milky-bland night sky of London. He would eegress this image as soon as he was reconnected. The stars became blurry, and he realized that he was crying. Another humiliation. He laughed dryly. If his fans could see him now.

Despite his fatigue, sleep wouldn't come. For hours he lay there, staring at the stars. Alone with his thoughts. Alone.

Totally alone.

*

He woke up to grey light, the pre-dawn sky cloaked with cloud. By habit, he ingressed the time and the weather, and of course, there was no response. He felt empty, morose. He was also thirsty, he realized. He sat up with a start. His hip-pack! He'd lost it somewhere – it could have been lost anywhere! He might have thrown it away when he panicked, or it could have fallen off, or he might have even lost it before the glitch happened, or perhaps he hadn't brought it at all. It didn't have much in it, four quarter-litre containers of energy drink – no: three; he remembered drinking one, so he must have had the pack at some time – and a couple of Nutrabars.

He sure could use one of those drinks now. He was probably hungry, too, but the thought of food wasn't appealing with his mouth so dry.

He couldn't just stay where he was, waiting; he had to take some action. Without any way of eegressing his predicament, there was no reason anyone would be looking for him, not for several days anyway. And then, where would they look? He had no idea where the transport had dropped him off, and no idea where he was supposed to rendezvous. With the connection, there'd been no reason to take note of such details. He was completely lost; he recognized nothing in his surroundings. He didn't even know if he should be heading to his left or to his right.

Priority for the moment: thirst. This wasn't an arid land; he often came across small streams of water running downhill. He stood up, warily, very conscious of the steep slope on either side of the path, but comforted by the trees. Again, without thinking intentionally, he ingressed for the weather, his position, a map of the area, locations of the provision huts . . . and of course nothing came to him.

He started along the path, continuing in the direction he'd been heading because it was as good a choice as any. Trees had fallen across the path in places; clearly, no one had been by to clear the trail for some time. After about 20 minutes, to his relief, the severity of the slope lessened. The woods ended, and he came to an area of gently rolling hills. The path bifurcated; for no particular reason, he chose the trail on the left rather than the one that turned abruptly downhill. He made similar intuitive decisions over the next hour or so as he tried to negotiate the complex trail system that spread web-like over the Fallowlands. Before the morning was half over, he had lost all sense of direction under the bright grey sky. Again and again, he ingressed for his location, for a map, for the direction to north, for the time, for the temperature, even for his mail and for the morning news. He ingressed the same way a man who has just lost an arm would still try to use it to reach for things. It was learned habit, not a conscious decision. His head began to ache so badly that he would stop and press the heels of his hands into his temples.

He finally came to a thin stream cutting across his path, 2 or 3 inches deep in places between head-sized stones. One could walk over it without getting one's feet wet. He knelt down quickly, cupped his hands, and brought some water to his mouth, then just lay down and immersed his face in the shallow water. "Oh, that's cold, that's beautiful," he said after he'd had a good drink, his face hovering above the water. He took a breath, then plunged his face again into the icy water. "Peter Piper picked a peck of pickled peppers," he said when he'd re-emerged. He laughed and rolled onto his back. "That makes absolutely no sense." He put his arm over his eyes. "I think I'm going insane," he said. "Insane, insane, insane." He sat up. "I think I'm going INSANE!" he shouted loudly at the mountains. "You *HEAR ME?*" He closed his eyes and squeezed his temples. "Insane, insane, insane . . ." His voice trailed off weakly. "How can anybody live like this? How can I . . ."

He took off his boots and his Fibre-Tec socks and stepped into the cold water. "Woo-hoo!" he exclaimed. "IT'S COLD!" he shouted to the mountains at the top of his lungs. "CAN ANYBODY HEAR ME? CAN ANY . . . Can any . . . anybody . . ." His voice trailed off again. He took another long drink, donned his footwear, and moved on.

With his thirst quenched, he directed his mind to two pressing needs: finding food and finding another human being. They didn't give out permits to the Central Europe Fallowlands in June; the hiking season (for the select few who *were* granted permits) was generally limited to July through September. Of course, with his ceeb status, he could get a permit to visit pretty well anywhere in the world, anytime he wanted. Well, his desire to be on his own for a few days without being hounded by fans and autograph hunters had certainly backfired on him, hadn't it? Still, there must be *some* people *somewhere* in the area, rangers, trail staff, another nature-loving ceeb with money or connections and a desire to be alone somewhere, no?

As for food . . . What was he supposed to do? Eat grass? Flowers? Was he supposed to hunt rabbits with his bare hands?

The connection *has to* come back soon, he told himself for the hundredth time. Once he had the connection back, a transport would be there in minutes.

He almost missed it: a patch of wild strawberries beside the path. They were red and tiny, smaller than the tip of his smallest finger. He plucked a couple and put them into his mouth. *Tasty,* he thought, but so minuscule they almost disappeared on his tongue before he could swallow anything. He knelt and began picking what he could find, using his right hand to take the berries and placing them in the palm of his left. Some were properly ripe, but most were red on one side and white on the other. He picked them anyway.

After a couple of minutes, the patch was exhausted of its supply. Tommy barely had a handful, about 20 berries. "More calories to pluck the bloody things than they're worth," he grumbled. He put the handful in his mouth all at once and swallowed the berries almost immediately.

A short distance along the trail, he found another patch, and then about an hour later a third. Each time he collected a handful, grumbled, and swallowed.

The trail he was following brought him closer and closer to a place where the green of the meadow ended, and the rock of the mountain rose skyward in front of him like a granite dinosaur. When it was clear that the path was going to greet the rock and not skirt it, he turned and retraced his steps to a previous junction, took a drink from the stream there, and chose a different way. Later, another trail he was on became a narrow path that crept along the upper edge of a deep chasm; Tommy immediately turned around and went back to find an alternate route.

The grey of the sky became more sombre, and by what he guessed was about mid-afternoon, a light rain began to fall. Tommy pulled the hidden hood of his AckerWear Ultra over his head. His outfit was waterproof. He certainly had serious problems, but dealing with the mild inconveniences of summer weather wasn't among them. He had passed the odd building from time to time – travellers' huts, dingy from months without use or cleaning and full of mouse droppings, a collapsing barn, a run-down boarded-up house – but he preferred to stay outside in the open on the chance that he might see someone.

The rain ended, and shortly before sunset, the fields filled with golden light. Ahead of him and to his left, perhaps 2 kilometres away, mountain rock surged upward, massive and irrefutable, scattering light with brushstrokes of red and orange, patches of white snow at elevation – and just a few metres in front of him was a goat. Tommy was almost upon the animal before he saw it. He stopped immediately.

This was food, part of his brain told him, the logical part that said a 280-pound man couldn't survive indefinitely on three handfuls of berries a day. Another part of his brain told him that food came in wrappers and neat packages, and meat, in particular, came in regular, organized, frying-pan-sized units, and needed to be cooked until it had just the right colour and texture – it certainly didn't come attached to living beings. There was a huge disconnect between the creature staring at him and what he needed to satisfy his growling stomach.

"Easy, boy," he said to the goat as he stepped slowly towards the animal. He intended to lay hold of it, rather uncertain of what he would do once he did. One thing at a time.

He got to within two steps when suddenly the goat pranced back, regaining its original distance. It lowered its head, looking at Tommy with steady, dark eyes. It was about waist high, with shaggy brown hair, black in places, and a four-inch black beard forming an isosceles triangle under its chin. Two horns curved straight back from its forehead, skimming a centimetre from the skull.

"Easy, boy, easy . . ." Tommy repeated as he approached the goat once more. The creature stared back, then teasingly jumped away again, this time uphill.

"Screw this." Tommy lunged at the goat, closing the distance in a heartbeat, and got hold of the animal's horns, rough against his hands. With unexpected strength and fury, the goat bucked and twisted and pulled, Tommy fighting to keep his grip and his balance. The two of them struggled evenly for a few seconds, with Tommy wondering what on Earth he was supposed to do next, when the goat suddenly lunged at *him*, becoming the aggressor. Tommy lost both grip and balance, falling down backwards on the slope. The goat stopped, levelling a threatening gaze at Tommy as if making a clear statement about who was boss here. Then it ambled a few steps up the hill and began eating the grass.

"Shit," Tommy said, picking himself up. An image came to his mind of a cowboy wrestling a steer to the ground in a rodeo. "Too tentative," he said to himself. "I have to use my strength and twist the thing. Get it on the ground and break its neck." This was the same part of his brain speaking that was telling him that the goat was food, and that killing animals was precisely how food was obtained. Voices from his ancestors were extolling him to be a hunter, to be a great hunter; it was in his blood. On the other hand, in *his* world, generations removed from his hunting forebears, he'd never killed anything bigger than an insect.

A third time Tommy approached the goat. The animal looked up, annoyed, and began ambling away slowly up the hill. The man increased his gait; the animal did the same, maintaining its distance. Tommy began to run, the goat also began a loping stride that seemed effortless, and then, suddenly, the creature about-faced and barreled down at Tommy with its head down, horns wielded like weapons, and the man had to sidestep nimbly to avoid being knocked over. They stared at each other for a few seconds, and then the goat lowered its head to charge again. "Shit!" Tommy said as he wheeled and ran. The goat took a few strides after him and then stopped.

Back at the path, Tommy turned to look upslope. The goat's eyes were on him, its black beard swaying side to side as it casually chewed a mouthful of grass. Then it began to slowly wander away. Tommy stayed put. He was hungry, but during his few seconds of wrestling with the goat, he realized that he wasn't hungry enough to really want to kill an animal and eat its raw flesh. He wasn't at that stage, not yet.

His body was tired, his mind more so. Even now, he found himself ingressing uselessly for time, weather, his heart rate. He sat down on the path, conscious of the aching hunger in his stomach, the ache in his head. He turned himself so that he was facing the rocky face of the nearby mountain, spectacular in its sheer immensity, shimmering against the evening sky. As the sun lowered, the colour muted from orange to magenta to fuchsia to violet, and finally it was just an immense darkness against the sky. Tommy lay down on the path, looking at the emerging stars.

"You know, goat, I'm gonna have some damn interesting experiences to eegress when I'm reconnected," he said quietly. "This must be some sort of record time away from the Hive. I can see the headlines on *Luker*. London e-news: 'TeePee Endures Three-Day Disconnect in Switzerland Fallows.' *New York InstaPress*: 'Football MVP Survives on Strawberries, Goatmeat.'" He sat up.

"YOU HEAR THAT, GOAT?" he shouted to the darkness. He lay down again, rubbed his eyes. "I'm going nuts." A minute later, he continued: "Yeah, I'm going nuts, but if I survive this thing, I'm gonna be making one whore of a lot more money."

If he'd been connected, someone would have chastised him for such a selfish thought, but for now, he was free to think what he wanted. And he found that oddly titillating.

*

Tommy woke up achy and depressed. He was thirsty, the emptiness in his stomach made him feel nauseous, and his head hurt. The sun hadn't risen yet, but the sky was blue and there were no stars. He considered the idea that he should find a stream and then just sit and wait there, rather than walking all over hell's half-acre. *Ah, I'll decide later.* He set off down the path, reasoning that with significant snow up above on the mountain there would likely be runoff streams not far ahead. *Figured that one all by myself.*

The trail entered a wooded area where the path was still damp from yesterday's rain. He saw some mushrooms, but didn't give the idea of eating them a second thought. Not without being able to ingress the *BOK* regarding edible and poisonous fungi, which he consciously avoided trying. In fact, other than the time and temperature when he first woke up, he hadn't attempted to ingress anything today.

The trail began a modest descent, and as it wrapped around a bulge of rock, he could only see the path about five paces ahead. To his right, the forest fell away steeply, and once again, he struggled to hold at bay his fear of heights. He hoped that this section was short. It was; after 30 metres the grade became far less severe, and the trail followed it downward with a large, looping S. At the bottom of the S was a person.

Tommy's eyes opened wide. "HEY!" he called, and he began running down the path, his relief pounding in his chest. "HEY!" Inexplicably, the figure slipped into the woods and disappeared. "HEY?" Tommy shouted, suddenly frowning. As he ran past the second loop of the S, he saw no one.

He stopped where he had last seen the figure. There was no sign of anyone.

"Hey, come back! Where are you? Where . . . where are you?

"*HEY!*" he shouted. He stood still and listened. He heard nothing. There wasn't much underbrush, and he could see perhaps 50 metres in each direction. The man couldn't have got very far, which meant that he must be hiding. And if he moved, Tommy would hear him.

Tommy forced himself to breathe slowly and quietly. There wasn't a breath of wind in the morning air. He scanned the area, thoroughly, and then scanned it again. Nothing but trees.

"Bloody imagination," Tommy mumbled. "I really am going nuts."

The crack of a gunshot exploded from the forest 20 metres away, and simultaneously he heard *THAK!* from a tree just behind his left shoulder.

"SHIT!" Tommy shrieked, and he instantly dropped to the ground, hugging the path with his whole body. The sound of the gunshot reverberated for several seconds, and then all was silent again.

He knew where the shot had come from; as he'd dropped, he'd seen a flash of colour from the direction of the sound. A shirt or something.

A Ketchen? Shit la merde, it's a frigging Ketchen! They really exist!

He made a quick lunge to the protection of a large stump nearby.

All he knew about Ketchen terrorists was that they were ruthless, murderous, and destructive. They were so small in number, so poorly organized, and basically so inept that in the large scheme of things, they were inconsequential, to the point where many people assumed they were a fictitious invention. Tommy himself didn't take half the stuff he saw in *Luker* seriously.

But right now, this wasn't exactly the large scheme of things, was it? Tommy took a piece of broken wood and threw it away to his left, and immediately darted to his right, cringing behind a tree just as another shot ran out, and then he sprinted behind a third tree. This one was a massive maple with a thick trunk. Tommy crouched and peered carefully around one edge. Through a bit of brush, he could see the man 10 metres away, rifle at his shoulder, bent low, creeping slowly forward. His black hair was tied behind his head, and he had dark brown eyes hooded with thick eyebrows so dense that they practically overlapped at the top of his hooked nose. His face was thin.

Tommy carefully removed his red jacket. Thank goodness for silent AckerWear Ultra zippers, he thought. He bundled the jacket. When the hooked-nosed man was about five steps away, Tommy threw the jacket away to his left, and as the man with the gun turned in that direction, Tommy sprinted out of cover towards him. Even weakened by almost three days without food, he was incredibly fast, and the man didn't have time to get the gun around before Tommy was upon him. A shot rang off, the bullet directed towards the upper branches of the tree as Tommy held the barrel with his left hand. The man might have been strong in his own right, but he was completely overpowered by six feet eight inches and 280 pounds of elite athlete. In seconds that were a blur, Tommy had the man on his back, the gun ripped from his hands, and he pummelled the smaller man as his fear was released explosively. Finally, he stood and lifted the man with a two-hand grip on the front of his shirt, then tossed him away as he would a doll.

He turned and picked up the rifle – the first time in his life he'd ever held a gun. He was breathing heavily, from emotion more than from exertion. He had no idea what he was going to do next.

The smaller man, stunned, slowly roused himself, turning on one side and propping himself on an elbow. He spat weakly, blood dribbling from his mouth. Then he turned towards Tommy. His eyes were defiant, even as a cheek ballooned to make one of them a slit. "Go ahead. Shoot me."

Tommy moved his lips, but nothing came out. The whole thing was just so preposterous. "What," he finally said, his face screwed up like a question mark, "what kind of asshole are you?"

The man on the ground leaned over his elbow and spat blood again. Then he turned back to Tommy. "Fuck you. Send that to your masters. Fuck all of you." Tommy said nothing. "You gonna stand there all day like a moron? Pull the fucking trigger. Fuckers."

What was he supposed to do? *What am I supposed to do! I need the connection! Please, somebody! I'm in the wilderness, lost, with a homicidal lunatic!*

What were his options? The man wasn't likely to help him out, bring him to food, call for a transport . . . So he could simply leave, taking the gun with him; he could hold the man as his prisoner; he could . . .

The man's open eye flickered at something involuntarily. Tommy felt his skin prickle. Was that a sound he heard behind him?

And then there was a flash of purple before his eyes as the blow to the side of his head knocked him into complete blackness.

2

Tommy was totally unaware of any passage of time between being knocked out and regaining consciousness. No dreams, no thoughts; it was like he was hit from behind, and then the next second, he was struggling to sit up. There seemed to be hands all over him, pulling him down to the surface he'd been lying upon. He opened his eyes, saw brightness, an unfamiliar room, half a dozen very agitated people, agitated because they were struggling against *him*, heard snippets of words and shouts, mostly in a language or in languages that he didn't understand, with the occasional phrase in English:

"... hold his arm ..."

"... strong bugger!"

"... get the needle ..."

"No, no needle. I want him awake." This from someone who was standing apart from the others.

Tommy was now fully roused, although thoroughly confused, and he began to fight his unknown assailants with a fury that was fuelled by his fear. In his disoriented bewilderment, all he could think about was escape. With a free leg, he kicked somebody in the chest; he got an arm loose and grabbed the cloth of someone's shirt, and then there were five people on top of him. Someone was trying to strap a leg to the table or whatever it was he was on; they were trying to strap his other limbs . . .

The table tipped over, and the chaotic struggle continued on the floor. A wave of pain in his head almost overwhelmed him, and for an instant his world was black again. Nevertheless, he kicked his legs free, flailed his arms, punched, elbowed, kneed – he was too powerful; they couldn't control him. He got to his feet, smashed a forearm into somebody's jaw, grabbed another by the cloth of the shirt and tossed him aside, felt the sickening wave of pain in his head again and almost fell over, took a step towards what he thought must be the door . . .

"Where are you going to go, Tommy?"

He stopped.

Once again the wave of pain, the colour of the room limited to shades of blue and grey . . .

Instantly hands were on him, pulling his arms . . .

"Let him go," the voice said, loudly but not crossly. Then, conversationally, "Where are you going to go, Tommy?"

Tommy stopped struggling; the hands reluctantly released him.

The man who had spoken, the one who'd been standing apart, now spoke calmly in a language Tommy thought was German. A couple of the people he'd been fighting answered back, one quite forcefully; the calm man replied, the other responded in apparent anger, the calm man replied again. He was clearly in charge. The angry man left with three of the others.

Tommy turned slowly. A wave of dizziness overwhelmed him, and he almost fell. The room seemed to be tilted. His head felt like it was about to explode.

"You'd better sit down, Tommy."

A chair materialized behind his knees; a hand was pushing him into it. He sat down and tried to relax his breathing. His dizziness waned, and the room returned to a semblance of focus.

"You've opened up where we'd stitched you." The man speaking looked to be about 70 years old. What was left of his hair was white and close-cropped, and he had arresting pale blue eyes magnified behind an enormous pair of glasses with heavy black frames. He was wiry and short, a full foot less than Tommy, and he wore a black beret. "Go get Ameline," he said to the person standing behind Tommy. "She's good at these things. Don't worry. I'm fine here with Mr. Antikagamac."

The old man stepped forward, righted the table that had fallen over, and then sat on its edge. "I'm sorry. My name is Lennox Voigt." He extended his hand.

Tommy ignored it. "Are you in charge here? What's going on? Why am I here?" The pain in his head when he spoke was so intense he was compelled to close his eyes. He put his hands to his head and felt wetness with his right. When he looked at it, it was covered with blood. That tempered his anger; in his gut, he felt the same fear he'd felt in the forest.

"Try to relax, Tommy." He took Tommy's clean hand and expertly felt for his pulse while he continued to speak. "Am I in charge? No. And yes. There's nobody who's really in charge, so to speak, but people tend to listen to me because I'm bald." He released Tommy's hand.

"You weren't connected when you stumbled upon Harrison, were you?"

Tommy didn't respond.

"A very fortuitous circumstance, for both of us. We would have had to uproot ourselves and move elsewhere. Ah: Ameline? I'd like you to meet Mr. Tommy Pierre Antikagamac. TeePee, as he's better known to his fans. Did you know Tommy is a quarterback for the London Knights, and that last year he was named the most valuable player in the World League of American Football?"

"Like I give a fuck about American football?" came a female voice with a French accent behind Tommy.

"I wish you would watch your language. You hang around Harrison too much. At any rate, it behooves us to be familiar with the enemy and its icons. Although I have to admit that it wasn't me who identified our guest. It was Myles."

"Self-adulating puppets. Sorry, Monsieur TeePee, but I'd rather puke than watch your sport."

Tommy winced as she applied pressure with something soft to the side of his head. "What's going on?" he asked again, quietly, almost mumbling. "What do you want with me?"

"Why were you disconnected?" Lennox asked.

"I don't know," Tommy muttered feebly. "It was a glitch." He felt a sharp sting on the side of his head; the woman was suturing his wound. He made an effort to remain stoic.

"The fact that the Mother still suffers glitches gives us all hope," Lennox said cryptically. "As I said: 'Lucky for you, lucky for us.' And lucky also that Harrison is such a lousy shot."

"Why am I here?"

Lennox removed his glasses and began cleaning them with a white cloth. "That is an excellent question. For those with a religious bent, your arrival may be seen as some sort of intervention by a divine providence. For those with a more mundane outlook, it's simply one random outcome of an infinite number of possibilities, a solution to a cosmic quantum equation, if you would. Otherwise known as a fortunate coincidence. 'Why,' you see, is a very deep question."

"Will you quit your bullshit and give me some sort of answer?" The woman was now repeating her procedure on the back of his skull. He realized to his surprise that his head hurt there as much as on the side. Which was odd because he hadn't been struck on the *back* of his head . . .

"I'm sorry; I'm in that kind of mood today. You deserve an explanation, but, to be frank, your mental state is rather fragile, as you are certainly aware. I suspect being part of the Hive leaves one woefully unprepared to think and to act on one's own." Lennox replaced his glasses. "Let me ask you: Do you know who we are?"

"Ketchen," Tommy answered. He wanted to add "despicable, murdering terrorists," but, given the fact that he suspected his captors were all madmen and just as likely to kill him as talk to him, he figured it was prudent not to say more than necessary.

"Not a name we give ourselves, but it will do. And what do you know of us?"

"Almost nothing."

"I'm sure you know much more than 'almost nothing.' You have a very strong mind, Mr. Antikagamac. You have been attached to the Mother for 20 years, and suddenly you are cut off. It is like someone who has had their legs braced all their lives, and one day the braces are removed. Does that person have the strength to walk? Does that person even know *how* to walk? Of course not.

"You are terrified right now. Terrified of the unknown, because there has never *been* an unknown for you before, and you are terrified of us, because we're what you call Ketchen. Despite this terror, which you feel right through your bones, you sit there, trying to look defiant, trying to look stable, when in your heart what you really want to do is curl up into a ball and cry. I'm impressed.

"Do you think we are terrorists?"

"Yes."

"What do you know of our cause?"

"Cause? You have no cause. You are anarchists; you want to destroy things."

"You probably get all your information on *Luker*. Tell me, Tommy, do you like thinking on your own?"

Tommy didn't understand the question.

"We've removed the braces on your mind."

Tommy felt a sting on the back of his head as the woman replaced another suture. "Look," he said, trying to keep his voice low enough to keep his head from splitting. "I've had enough bullshit. I want you to tell me, right now, what the hell is going on and what do you want with me?"

"Tommy, there's no longer 'us' and 'you.' You are now one of us."

Tommy stared at the man with the glasses, uncomprehending. Then he slowly moved his hand to feel the back of his head where the woman had finished replacing the sutures. And a small sound, a kind of croak, escaped unbidden from his lips as he recognized the true horror of the situation.

3

Somehow, he had to get out of there, make his way back to civi-lization . . . have the connection repaired . . . They'd destroyed it! These sociopaths, these primitive . . . *animals*! He had no hope now of the Mother connecting with him, even when they repaired the glitch. How could he get back on his own? How could anyone find him?

He was well-guarded; day or night someone with a rifle was always present. They'd quartered him in a large tent, heavy canvas on strong poles, rectangular in shape and tall enough that even Tommy could stand inside and walk around. It was furnished, if you could call it that, with a cot, a table, a supply cupboard, and three chairs. On the occasions when he'd been escorted to the latrine, he'd seen a dozen other tents, several considerably bigger, some with electricity, laid out helter-skelter over a hectare under the forest cover. There may have been other tents beyond his limited sightline.

Once he tried to ask the guard about the location of this "outpost," but the guard didn't speak any English, except to say,

"No Englich, no speck." *Figures,* Tommy thought sullenly. They're a bunch of Neanderthals. With the Hive, everyone in the whole world could communicate with everyone else. If someone didn't speak English, which was rare, Canspik could provide instantaneous translation. But here? *No Englich, no speck.*

Lennox came by quite frequently.

"How are you feeling, Tommy?"

"Piss off."

"Is that your own thought? If it is, then: good. You're making progress. But I fear it's just an echo in your mind from the collective wisdom of the Hive. To think of the intellectual achievements of humanity, Chaucer and Shakespeare and Dickens, to name three men of the word from your adopted country, and the Hive spews out 'Piss off.' It's rather sad.

"You're so much better off now."

The girl called Ameline came by from time to time. She was a short girl, late twenties or early thirties, with brown hair tied into a pony-tail. Her teeth were crooked; obviously, she'd never had braces when she was a kid. The bridge of her nose was a bit sunken, making it rather more concave than a plastic surgeon would be comfortable with. Tommy wondered if it had been broken at one time. Nevertheless, she was healthy and youthful, and pretty enough despite her facial defects.

"Do you enjoy mathematics, Monsieur Antikagamac?"

A rather bizarre start to a conversation, Tommy thought. With her French accent, "mathematics" was pronounced "matematic." "No, I don't particularly. And you can call me Pierre. That's my name, Tommy Pierre. My grandmother was French Canadian, you know."

"Ah, oui, j'avais oublier. 'TeePee.' C'est stupide. Et vous pouvez parler français?"

"No. I, ah, my mother spoke a bit. So, do you enjoy football?"

"Don't be an idiot. Can you multiply 11 by 14?"

Tommy failed to suppress a derisive laugh. "Sure."

"*Et . . .*"

"Look, my head's still hurting. Don't make me laugh. I'm not in the mood."

"I have no cares for your moods, Monsieur Antikagamac. Eleven by fourteen? I wait your answer."

"I don't know," Tommy answered irritably. "Who cares?"

"You should care, Monsieur Antikagamac. You should care that you never learned how to think."

"I can think just fine, thank you. Eleven by fourteen isn't thinking. That's what's known as a low-level machine operation. If you call that 'thinking,' then you don't really understand the word. It's demeaning, not to mention woefully inefficient. How about 569.5 divided by 13.4? I'd have the answer in a picosecond. You" – he almost added the word "savages," but caught himself – "can waste your mental energy on such mundane things as multiplying numbers together; with the Hive our minds are free to contemplate issues of a higher nature."

"Like American football."

"It sure beats what's going on around here."

"Monsieur Antikagamac . . ."

"Pierre."

"Monsieur Antikagamac, we have to wash your brain, you know? *Se laver.* The only way to wash a brain is to think. Think, think, think." She tapped her temple with her index finger. "Scrub, scrub, scrub. What is two by five?"

Tommy made a sound like he was spitting. "Ten."

"Three by six."

"Ah, this is stupid."

"Three by six?"

"Piss me off. Eighteen."

"Good. Nine by seven?"

"Enough, already!"

"Nine by seven?"

"I don't care what nine by seven is! Look, my head's pounding; why don't you just leave me alone."

"I will stop after this one. Nine by seven."

"Shit. Fifty . . . uh, hell, I don't know. Fifty-six."

"It is not 56. Monsieur Antikagamac, your brain is weak, and it is full of crap. I will come back in two days. Maybe you will be more ready to clean out your brain then. I hope that you will not be too hungry when I come because the guard will not give you food until you tell him the answer to nine by seven."

"Aw, piss off! Why doesn't everybody just *piss off*!" He put his hands over his eyes. He was sure his head was going to split in two. He heard Ameline speaking to the guard just outside his tent in German.

"Oh, and Monsieur Antikagamac?" she said from the entrance. "The answer is 42.5."

Tommy looked up with a pained, questioning grimace.

"Five hundred sixty-nine point five divided by thirteen point four."

*

On the fourth, or maybe it was the fifth, day of his confinement, he was sitting on the edge of his cot with his hands over his eyes when he heard a tentative tap on the wooden beam beside his tent entrance. He looked up to see a woman standing there, smiling benevolently, with a small pack over her shoulder. With her kind face and mild demeanour, she reminded Tommy of a volunteer collecting for charity. She was perhaps in her mid-fifties, with hair that was equal parts blond and grey.

"Good morning, Tommy. My name is Frenna. Frenna Gurdwald. May I come in?" She spoke with only a slight trace of a German accent.

Tommy shrugged and lazily indicated one of the chairs. He remained where he was.

"Thank you. My goodness, you are a big man! Forgive me, but it's the first time I have seen someone bred for American football. I like sports. I used to play football when I was younger, but, of course, it was the World variety, you know with the round ball that you just kick. I know it's no longer very popular in the world of the Hive, but among the Freemen we still play.

"How are you doing? How is your head?"

"Okay," he said without embellishment. In reality, he was bored, and his depression was deepening. The silence in his mind was like a suffocating blanket. No news, no chat, nothing to occupy his restless thoughts. He couldn't even play games. As for his head, the pain was still there, less intense, but definitely still there. He had trouble sleeping.

"I'm sure it still hurts. I won't stay very long. Tommy, do you know how to read?"

He groaned inwardly. *Not more of this!* "Of course."

"Good! Can you tell me what types of things you like to read? Your favourites?"

He considered making a sarcastic response, but her friendliness was disarming. Instead, he answered truthfully.

"I read the news. You know, *Luker.* And sports stories. And science fiction."

"Oh, I like science fiction also. I'm a big fan of Ray Bradbury. Have you read Ray Bradbury?"

"No, I don't think so." In truth, he'd never heard of Ray Bradbury. "I don't want to keep you. I thought you might like to read something, so I've brought some books for you to choose from. I really didn't know what you might like." She pulled the pack from her shoulder and, opening it, withdrew a half-dozen books which she set on the ground at Tommy's feet.

Tommy looked at them as he would an exotic animal. He'd never seen a paper-book before that wasn't under glass in a museum. They weren't even legal. He struggled to read the titles on the covers; it was a difficult chore without the connection. He picked up one of them gingerly, the way he would a baby bird. His lips moved involuntarily as he read the title.

"*Watership Down*," Frenna said with a smile. "I loved that book when I was a child. Have you read it?"

Tommy shook his head no. He flipped carefully through some pages. It was almost all writing, with occasional black and white drawings of rabbits. *This is as primitive as cave markings*, he said to himself. "So, when you 'read a book,' this is all you have? You read all the words and look at the pictures?"

"What else would there be?"

"When *we* read a book," – he was referring to those who were connected to the Mother, which pretty well encompassed everybody on the planet except for the Ketchen – "the whole thing is displayed with rich colour and sounds and music, almost like real life, except better."

"The book is displayed on a wall?"

"No, no. It's in your head. I don't think I can explain it. You put on the eye and ear blocks, so there's no distraction (at least, you would for a book; if it's just the news or a short blurb, you wouldn't bother), you choose what you want to read – every book that's ever been constructed is available – you choose your version, because there's often a choice, and then you just relax and watch, listen, and feel. It's wonderful. And the technology is getting better all the time. They're working on a system that will allow you to actually become one of the characters. It's really an amazing experience. This . . ." – he held up the book – "Do you have to go through it and actually read all the words?"

"My goodness, Tommy Pierre, what you call reading isn't reading at all! Reading is something that you do, not something that is done *for* you. You read the book and form your *own* images as you go along. And, yes, it is an amazing experience."

Tommy opened to the first page and slowly read the first couple of sentences. "Seems terribly boring," he said. "It takes forever to read just a bit. How long does it take to read a book like this?"

"Oh, I'd spend a week or two, depending on how much time I get to sit and relax . . ."

"Pah! With the connection, I can read a book in a couple of hours."

"But it's not reading."

"Of course it is. Look, I don't rub sticks together to make a fire, you know what I mean? We've progressed far beyond reading paper-books filled with script. And it's like that with everything, not just books. We're so much more advanced. I don't understand why you people are bent on destroying everything. It makes no sense. No sense at all." He wanted to get angry, but a combination of overwhelming fatigue and Frenna's apparently honest friendliness prevented him.

"Give it time, Tommy Pierre." She could have been his mother. "At any rate, you've got no choice. Why don't you keep that book – read it when you feel like it. I'll come back; you can tell me what is happening in the story. I would like that."

When she had gone, Tommy sat on his cot once again with his head in his hands. After a while, he picked up the book and stared at its cover. *Watership Down.* Opening the cover, he saw a note written in pen on the inside. "Dear Felix: I hope this helps with your study of English. Happy eleventh birthday. Mama."

4

As the wounds on his head healed and the headaches and concussion symptoms abated somewhat, he became more accustomed to the profound emptiness in his mind. Agitation and incomprehension and insecurity gave way to bitter loneliness. It wasn't just the fact that he was a prisoner, cut off from the people he knew, cut off from the 20 primary contacts and 3 000 secondary contacts that he would normally communicate with in the course of a day, cut off from the world he knew. It was the way his thoughts just bounced around inside his head, with nowhere to go. Thoughts without purpose.

He slept a great deal. Whereas the first few days he had trouble sleeping at all, now he typically slept for 13 or 14 hours at a time. He couldn't remember his dreams when he woke up, except that they had been disturbing. When he was awake, he was restless, often pacing his tent relentlessly, as if he were in a hurry to go somewhere. The dimness of the tent, hidden as it was in the perpetual shadow of the forest, had been a blessing his first few days, but now that he was more tolerant to light, he found it depressing.

He asked for, and was given, an electric lamp which he kept on whenever he wasn't sleeping. He tried reading the book to give himself something to do, just a little bit at a time, but he found the exercise difficult and exhausting. On his first attempt, in fact, he gave up before he had finished a page, tossing the book away in frustration and cursing the inefficiency of reading blocks of written words. When Frenna came by, she seemed honestly disappointed that he had given up on it, and Tommy felt compelled to try again.

For about an hour a day, he did a physical exercise routine, limited in scope to what he could do inside the tent, and odd because he had no feedback as to heart rate, oxygen consumption, blood pressure, lactic acid concentration, and a dozen other metabolic indicators that he would normally monitor while he trained. There was usually an audience at the open front of his tent: the guard, of course, but other people would come by and watch for a few minutes before continuing with their business. He didn't mind; after all, his career was based on people coming to watch him perform. If these people got a kick out of seeing him do hand-stand push-ups without his shirt, let them. To his surprise, he noted that one of the observers, standing quite far back from the others, was a little girl of about 10 years of age. She was the only child he'd seen since being captured, and when he stopped to look at her, she ran off.

He craved stimulus. He asked to go to the latrine more often than necessary, just to get out of his tent and smell the breeze. He even tolerated Ameline's visits with her annoying mathematics lessons. Truth be told, they weren't annoying at all; his brain seemed to be itchy, and thinking mathematics, elementary as it was, soothed it in some weird, unexpected fashion.

Her lessons were always three parts. First, there was simple arithmetic, such things as multiplying and dividing numbers, then came algebra, and she finished off the lesson with geometry. She would bring sheets of paper, all of them marred from having become wet at some time in the past, and pencils. Tommy would smirk ironically at the thought that he was in a 1900s-era schoolroom. And while one part of his head found the whole idea pointless and degrading – "Time for our daily bullshit?" became his regular greeting to Ameline – another part revelled in the construction and organization of mathematical concepts. For her part, Ameline never failed to call him "pathetic" or "sorry" or "*une chèvre*," which he found out later was a goat.

*

"Hey! Guard!"

The man with the rifle sidled up to the screen door of Tommy's tent.

"Me want walk." Tommy used two fingers to simulate a person walking along his arm. "Want go walkie, understand?"

"I speak English," the guard said with a German accent. "You vant to use ze latrine?"

"No, I'm sick of walking to the latrine. I'm sick of this tent. I'm sick of the smell. I'm sick of the view. I want to go somewhere. Anywhere."

"You iss only allowed to go to ze latrine."

"That's asinine. This whole thing is asinine. You're just standing out there, watching me stand in here. Listen. I go for a walk, and you follow behind me with your gun. What's the difference? I run, you shoot me. Think of it as a walk to the latrine, except longer."

The guard said nothing, just gazed back steadily, until Tommy began to think that he hadn't understood a thing. Tommy was about to shake his head and mutter an expletive when the guard turned and whistled three sharp notes. Some moments later, a second man appeared in front of the tent. The two conversed in German, then the second man disappeared.

"What's happening?" Tommy asked.

"Your reqvest iss being considered."

My reqvest iss being considered, Tommy thought caustically. *Shit la merde.* He walked back to his bed and sat down heavily.

He had to get out. Before he suffocated; before he ran out of room to move. The space within his tent was getting smaller each day. He was sure of it. He'd taken to measuring the distance from one side to another, and though it remained seven and one-third paces, he knew that each day it was less than it had been the previous day. Even now, he felt the walls pressing inward.

He had to get out. Maybe he would just get up, go out the door, and walk away. See what they do. Let them shoot him if they wanted. What did he have to lose? That's it. He was going to get up and walk out, and the guard might as well shoot him because he wasn't stopping.

Still, he sat there.

Presently, the guard came up to the screen. "All right, mein friend. Come."

Tommy didn't let the relief show on his face.

As he stepped outside, he saw that there was a second man, also armed with a rifle, standing to the side, about 5 metres away. "Follow me," the first man said.

The three set out, Tommy following the guard he'd spoken with, and the third man five paces behind Tommy. The initial steps took Tommy along a familiar path, and he feared for a moment that they *were* just taking him to the latrine. But then they stepped off to the side, and Tommy found himself along a new and less worn trail. He breathed a sigh of relief. For the first time in what seemed a very long time, he felt free to stand tall, to stretch out his shoulders, and he realized that he had been holding himself in a hunch ever since he had been in confinement. He let his chest expand as his lungs pulled summer air in through his nose, air thick with the fragrance of fungus and moss. It was a clear day, and in places where the tree cover was thin, sunlight dappled the ground.

The trail was hardly worth that name; it was wild and uneven, and if Tommy had been alone, he would have had trouble following it. After about 10 minutes of walking, the little there was of the trail petered out. The three men split up, Tommy continuing straight ahead through an area of thin underbrush, with the other two half a dozen metres to his left and to his right (but with rifles always pointed towards Tommy), and they proceeded this way for about 50 metres. There they came to a more established trail, of the type Tommy had been following before he'd been captured. They resumed their initial formation: Tommy two paces behind the man who had been guarding his tent, the other armed man five paces farther back.

"What's your name?" Tommy asked the man in front.

"Karl Schreibert," the guard answered.

"So, Karl Schreibert, what do you do here other than guard the occasional prisoner?"

"I doodle eqvations relating to ze qvantum gravity in N dimensions. Zat is, ven I am not peeling potatoes." He said something in German to the other guard, and the two of them laughed.

After that, they continued in silence. Tommy felt his depression returning. He was outside, finally away from the vicinity of his tent, but the trail, the trees, the flora – it seemed so unexpectedly, so disappointingly, *boring*. The exercise was good, but the walk was tedious. *There should be more than this*, he thought. He loved the outdoors, at least, he *used to* love the outdoors. It was in his blood; it was somewhere in his ancestry. That was one of the reasons he escaped from the city when he could, and every June used his ceeb privileges to go to places like the Fallowlands where he could feel particularly close to nature. He would run, train, explore, camp out . . . and everywhere he went, he would, with the help of the BOK, identify flowers and insects and trees and anything else his eyes spotted or his ears heard or his nose sensed. He eegressed his experiences constantly and instantly. His contacts were immediately aware of his thoughts, the sights he was seeing, the sounds he was hearing, the emotions he was feeling. The world was rich, and his connection to the Hive brought him right into the midst of it, and with him everyone with whom he wished to share his thoughts.

But now he was alone. The input from his senses bounced around in his head and disappeared unheard, unshared. As he walked along, he saw mushrooms and flowers, and that's all they were: mushrooms and flowers. He knew nothing. He was an outsider, looking at the world dully, as if through bad optics, as if it were black and white when it should have been brilliant colour. He smelled the breeze: nothing came to his mind. He wasn't a sentient being; he was a shadow.

Karl raised his hand, signalling that they should stop.

"What . . ." Tommy started, but Karl shushed him with some urgency. The man following said something quietly to Karl, and the two Germans exchanged words in hushed tones. Karl reached down and touched the bark of a tree beside the trail at about knee level, and then rubbed his fingers together. Then he continued walking forward, but at a much slower pace than before. He was clearly looking for something.

"Please valk qvietly, and don't speak," he said softly to Tommy.

They walked this way for the next several minutes, Karl occasionally pausing to look deeper into the forest undergrowth to his left or down onto the trail at his feet. Sometimes he exchanged a word with the other guard. At one point, they changed places, the German who spoke no English taking the lead. Twice they stopped completely, and Tommy waited with anxious curiosity as the guard in front left the trail to examine something on the forest floor.

Finally, the leading guard put up his hand firmly. "Stay here," Karl said quietly from behind. "If you move, ve vill kill you." The two Germans moved stealthily into the forest, about 15 metres apart from each other, leaving Tommy alone on the trail. *They're hunting something*, Tommy thought, but he had no idea what. He saw nothing but trees and a forest floor strewn with evergreen needles and decaying logs covered with moss. *Now!* His brain shouted when they were a short stone's throw away. *Now! Run!* With his speed, he could be beyond their ability to shoot him in seconds. *Why wasn't he moving?* He remained rooted to the ground, frozen in the place Karl had told him to stay. Was he afraid? No, he knew he could make it. His paralysis was rooted in something else, something he couldn't grasp. *Now! Now! Go!* Still he didn't move. Absurdly, the rabbits of *Watership Down* came to his mind, Hazel and Fiver and Bigwig, and for a split second and to his utter astonishment, he realized that he didn't want to *share* his vision of rabbits with his thousand Hive contacts, because they were *his* rabbits . . .

The report of a gunshot startled him. At the same instant, there was movement, a hysterical squealing sound that came from the living black mass that had suddenly appeared and was racing deeper into the forest, and then there was a second report, and the creature dropped and lay still.

41

Karl hurried to where their quarry had fallen, while the other German immediately turned his weapon towards Tommy. His split second of hesitation had cost him his chance to escape.

Karl stood up with a huge smile. "Come here, Herr Tommy. Ve hass just shot our supper."

A half-hour later, Tommy held one end of a large sturdy branch on one of his shoulders, and in front of him, the German who spoke no English held the other end. Between them, the boar hung, a hundred kilograms of beast suspended by its hooves, which had been expertly tied together. Karl followed, his rifle ready. And Tommy just wanted to get back to his tent and put his head in his hands.

5

$$(3x + 5)(5x + 12)$$

It was one of a series of exercises that Ameline had written for Tommy to solve. He was sitting at a small wooden table with folding legs in an open area a short distance from his tent. A man stood nearby, shirt sleeves rolled up, holding a rifle loosely. A squirrel chattered from a branch of a nearby tree.

Recently, he had been allowed out for short periods of time, at first with two armed guards watching him, but now one seemed to suffice. Truth be told, his desire to flee was not as paramount as it had once been. Oh, he still thought of escape, but not to the point where he would risk dodging a bullet to get out of there. Things continued to change in his head. The silence was no longer an agony; the fact was that he had come to be rather comfortable with it, although that fact, in itself, made him feel uneasy. As for re-establishing contact with his friends: it would be nice to communicate with them, but, again, the desire wasn't as compelling as he thought it should be. As things stood now, he seemed willing to wait a bit longer, to see where things here were headed. They couldn't keep him a prisoner indefinitely, and they certainly didn't seem to want to harm him any more than they'd already done.

Sunlight through the trees dappled the surface of the paper. Ameline herself had slipped away for some reason or another, leaving Tommy alone with his guard for a few minutes while he worked. He breathed deeply through his nose, savouring the wild scent of forest air, exhaling through his mouth. He flicked away an ant that was walking along on his paper and wrote

$$15x^2 + 61x + 60.$$

He smiled and stretched his arms over his head before continuing to the next question on the paper. As he stretched, he noticed the little girl he'd seen before staring at him from a distance of several metres. He lowered his arms and stared back. He made a mean face at the girl. She responded by also making a mean face. He made his meaner, and she did likewise. It was a game.

"*Vanessa! T'en aller! Vite!*"

Ameline entered the open area shooing the little girl, who disappeared into the trees like a chipmunk.

"Who's the girl?" Tommy asked.

"She is my daughter."

Tommy raised his eyebrows in surprise. *Your daughter?* "Ameline" and "mother" would never have been associated in his mind of their own accord. "Is she registered?" he blurted out stupidly, then instantly answered his own question: "Of course not. None of you are registered."

"Registered?" Ameline said derisively. "No, I'm not *registered*. Vanessa is not *registered*. Fuck *registered*."

"Yeah, well *you* can 'fuck registered'; for the rest of the world, it's a necessary sacrifice we make to keep the planet viable. If we were selfish enough to have babies willy-nilly, there'd *be* no more Fallowlands or any other lands for you and your girl, or for anybody."

"Yes, right. Thank you very much, Monsieur TeePee. You have saved the world for everybody." She curtsied sarcastically.

"Bloody well right. You know, maybe it's time for me teach *you* a little mathematics. And a little history.

"Did you know that before the war, there were 10 billion people on this planet? Ten billion. Getting bigger all the time. And the Earth is a sphere, right? $4\pi R^2$, right? And R is constant, no? Wait: something wrong with the math. Not enough space. Not enough food. Not enough air, water. Not enough *anything*, except garbage and excrement.

"War comes. Ten billion minus two billion equals eight billion. Eight billion the $4\pi R^2$ can handle, if things are organized properly. So calculations are made, hard decisions are made, and people go along with the hard decisions because it's hard to ignore the testimony of 2 billion fresh graves. The great Farmbelts are created, large swaths of Canadian prairie, Russia, Argentina, Malaysia, and so on, nothing but high-efficiency farming, enough to feed 8 billion. The Fallowlands: central Europe, which was a mess after the war, the Amazon, Asian tundra, Africa, half a dozen others, so that the planet can breathe. And with what's left, there's really plenty of space for 8 billion people to live quite comfortably. But the equation doesn't hold, unless the 8 billion is a constant, just like R is. How do you keep 8 billion a constant? $C - A + A = C$, no? So: everybody is registered, and if you want to have a child, you fill out an application. A computer algorithm assures that birth permits are granted fairly, under the overriding requirement that the number of new births matches the number of deaths. $C - A + A = C$. That, my dear, is mathematics."

"And suppose I make love with my husband, and we have a child: in your world, I am now a criminal?"

Tommy shook his head condescendingly. He was enjoying being the teacher for a change. "Children aren't conceived that way anymore. Females are . . . well, 'zigged' is the common word; I forget the medical term for it. Anyway, this is done before puberty. When a birth permit is granted, then the woman can provide her own egg, or use somebody else's, and likewise, the couple can use the man's sperm or somebody else's. It has nothing to do with intercourse. Once the fetus is started and everything looks healthy, then the woman can decide if she wants natural childbirth or incubation. Most choose incubation these days, but you still get some women who want to go the natural route.

"So you see, sex and procreation have been completely decoupled. Women and men are inherently equal. All babies are wonderfully healthy. The population remains stable and functional. The planet is also healthy, with all its ecosystems intact. It's all very logical." Tommy leaned back in his chair, quite proud of his brief and lucid lecture.

"You live in a bullshit world," Ameline said with disgust.

"Well, do you have any better ideas?" Tommy came back angrily. "Go ahead, you're the mathematics genius. How do *you* keep human beings from overpopulating the Earth?"

"I don't know. But this is bullshit. Let's stop talking. You have exercises to perform."

She sat down and picked up a paper that Tommy had already completed. Tommy continued his work.

"So," he said after a minute, without looking up, "you have a husband?"

"No."

Tommy continued to work on his exercises, but he found his concentration waning. More than once, he glanced at Ameline from beneath his eyebrows. *She's a fireball,* he thought. He found himself smiling as he looked back to his exercise.

"I had a husband," Ameline said without prompting, also keeping her eyes down on the page she was correcting. "He was captured. By your people. When one of us is captured, we all have to flee to a new place. Because your Hive eats his brain and they know everything. Vanessa was five."

Tommy's smile disappeared.

"I think we've had enough for today." Ameline got up abruptly and left the area without looking back.

*

Several times each day, he would pick up the book and read. At first, it was just a paragraph or two; that was all he could take before his concentration waned and his head began to hurt. He had trouble visualizing what the words were describing. It was work. Then Frenna would come by, and they would talk about what he'd read, and the rabbits of *Watership Down* would come alive, a small band of long-eared, vulnerable rabbits on a perilous journey through the English countryside. Sometimes Frenna would read four or five pages aloud while Tommy listened – and he was amazed, not only at the images that came to his mind, but how easily they came, and what a kick he got from those images. So different, so primitive compared to the brilliant Technispectral images he would normally be watching when he read a book, but these were . . . his own, from his own brain, and somehow that made them special, even if they were vague and incomplete.

And then there was Frenna herself. She affected him in a strange way, leaving him anxious and uncertain.

His communication with her was so different than his communication had been with his contacts, even his close contacts, within
the Hive. It was less, and more, at the same time. That didn't make
sense, of course, but what in his brain did make sense these days?
He tried with some desperation to understand what was going
on in his head, but it was like trying to catch fog. He knew that
when he was face to face with Frenna, he felt a certain richness
in the communication that he simply didn't experience when he
was face to face with a friend in the Hive. Perhaps it was because
hers was the only voice, and the communication was sustained
for a significant length of time without interruption. Both points
were a significant departure from typical Hive conversation. He
suspected, however, that it was something more than that.

On the other hand, when he was away from a contact in the
Hive, he could still communicate, with all the effort of a thought.
When Frenna was gone, in contrast, communication dropped to
zero. If he wanted to tell her about something he'd just read that
he found striking, he couldn't. If he had a question, it had to wait.
The highs and lows perceived from a friend's presence or absence
were dramatically more pronounced here than in the world he
was used to.

Lennox, Ameline, the others with whom he'd had limited conversations: they also affected him, but to a lesser degree. If he was
going to figure out what was going on in his mind, the key right
now was Frenna.

There was something else that he was finding intriguing: his
thoughts were his own.

As part of the Hive, his thoughts were available to everyone. It
was no big deal; it was just how life worked. Your thoughts were
always accessible, if anyone was interested enough to ingress
them. Of course, for him, as one of the world's most high-profile

ceebs, his thoughts were ingressed by millions every day. Again, so what? You got used to it. And you always had the ability to temporarily block things from the general public or from an individual or a set of individuals – a surprise gift for your mother or a football play from the opposing team, for example – as long as the block was approved and the thought monitored. It was a learned ability, something that happened at the speed of thought and at a deep, internal level, no different than commanding the sequencing of neuron firings that enabled your right leg to take a step while walking.

But here no one was checking his thoughts. He found that really weird. And now that he'd grown accustomed to that . . . privacy, he guessed it would be called . . . he found he liked it. He really liked it. And he found the fact that he liked it very disturbing.

*

Lennox examined the area where the wounds on the side and, particularly, the back of Tommy's head, had healed. He used a lens of some sort to focus light into his eyes. He felt his pulse at his neck.

"You're a doctor?" Tommy asked, as Lennox pressed his ear into Tommy's back.

"I've read some books. Breathe deeply."

"Real encouraging."

"Breathe again."

"If you were connected to the Mother, you would have access to every medical article ever written. Not to mention that you could examine me a whole lot better than you are doing now with both of us sitting at home."

"Very interesting. Lie on your back."

"When's the rain supposed to stop?"

"It's here for most of the day, I figure. You're going to tell me that with the connection I could find out when it would stop to the nearest minute."

"What, you think the weathermen are miracle workers? Probably only the nearest 10 minutes. Frustrating as hell."

"When did you break your rib?"

"Three years ago. Week 12, fourth quarter. Madrid Toreadors. We were up 21–17. We ended up losing by a field goal."

"How are the headaches?"

It took Tommy a second to realize that the question referred to the present time. "Pretty well gone. I usually feel funny when I wake up in the morning, but it goes away after a while."

"Are you still sleeping 12 hours?"

"At least. I used to get by on six."

"That's fine. For now, it's good for you. You can sit up." Lennox himself sat in a chair opposite, removed his glasses, and began to clean them with a white cloth. "I think, Tommy, that you are officially healed from your concussion. You're healthy as an ox; frankly, I've never met anyone who had a resting heart rate of 46. As for the other thing . . ." He shrugged his shoulders, replaced the glasses on his nose. He looked at Tommy intently. "Are you making progress?"

A week ago, Tommy would have jumped upon that question, and in fact had done so, saying, "I'm sick of being in this tent. I'm sick of being a prisoner. I'm sick of not knowing what you want or why I'm here. I'm sick of you. I'm sick of the guard. I just want to get out of this asylum and back to some semblance of civilization and sanity! That's my progress!"

But now he was much more reflective. Things were changing in his head . . . he had thoughts that nobody else knew about, and he found a guilty pleasure in that, and he wasn't sure why he felt guilty. There was emptiness where there should have been input from his friends, his contacts . . . again, that feeling that *something wasn't right!* because he found the emptiness satisfying.

"I don't know," he said after a few moments. "It's so different. I . . . It's . . . I was listening to the rain yesterday . . . just listening. I've listened to rain before – hell, a quick check of Soundscape and I could have told you the size of the raindrop and the surface it was landing on – but this was different. I was listening, and that was all. I didn't want to check anything. Boring, simple, unenhanced rain, and I stood listening to it and nothing more for . . . who knows? Ten minutes? I would have never wasted 10 minutes like that before. Is that progress, or regression? I don't know anymore. I have thoughts, but I don't know what to do with them. I feel like all this energy in my brain is going nowhere. It's not just undirected thought, it's *pointless* thought. Sixteen times 25 is 400, but so what? I'm reading this book, the story goes so slowly, I get these images but how am I supposed to know if they are the right ones . . ."

"Was it pleasant?" Lennox interrupted.

"What?"

"Listening to the rain."

Tommy shrugged. "I suppose. Yeah, I guess it was in some feeble way, but that's precisely what I find disturbing: I should be doing something much more consequential with my brain than pointlessly . . . what: existing? I mean, here it's okay because there's not a witch's wart else to do, but if I've lowered my mental functions so much that doing nothing and thinking about nothing is enough to give me satisfaction . . . I'm scared. I'm scared that my mind is just deteriorating. I'm regressing. Perhaps that's the progress you want. Perhaps that's just what you people are hoping for."

"And if you'd been connected to the Hive? I know, you wouldn't have spent 10 minutes listening to the rain. But if you had? And you found it enjoyable? Then what?"

"I'd share it, of course. I'd eegress my thoughts to my contacts, and we'd share it. This . . . here . . . I couldn't share with anybody, except to tell you in words, and the words are like nothing compared to the thoughts!"

"And so, you 'eegress' your thoughts, your 'pleasure' to your friends. Forgive me, but I'm curious. What then? Do your friends share your pleasure?"

"Of course." Tommy snorted a short laugh. "And then someone would eegress the sound of rain falling in the Amazon. Or on the Pacific Ocean." Tommy paused and rubbed his temples. With a smaller voice, he said, "And this little sound-thought would be so pale by comparison that it wouldn't be worth anything."

Lennox didn't respond, other than to smile faintly as he regarded Tommy with an intensity that was unnerving, his eyes magnified by the converging lenses of his glasses. After a moment, he brought his hands together at his face, enclosing his nose, and proceeded to stare at his knees.

As Tommy had answered the question about his progress, his mood had changed from upbeat to depressed in only a few moments. Now, as he looked at Lennox in the chair opposite, staring at his knees with his hands enclosing his nose, the thought that crept into his head was: *These people are alien. What have I descended to?*

After several seconds, Lennox stood up abruptly. "Come with me. We're going for a little walk." Immediately, he turned and exited the tent.

Tommy followed; wearing only a shirt on top, he quickly became wet with warm rain. Lennox was a few steps ahead, wearing a leather jacket with no hood. The guard with the gun followed Tommy alertly, but Lennox stopped and spoke to the guard in German. A heated exchange ensued, and they were soon joined by two other men who came from nearby tents. The three men and Lennox were clearly in sharp disagreement about something, and Tommy guessed that *he* was the something. In time, the arguing ceased, and Lennox turned to Tommy with a light smile.

"Come along."

Tommy followed Lennox along a path that skirted past several of the tents. When he looked back, he saw that the guard with the gun had stayed behind, the three men conversing animatedly while watching him and Lennox intently. Presently, a turn in the path left them out of sight.

Lennox was talking, turning back to Tommy from time to time as he walked ahead. "The Freemen, what's left of us, are the remnants and the descendants of those who were never connected to the Hive. Even before it became law, of course, there were very few who'd resisted the frenzy to become connected – certainly less than one percent of the whole population. But then it became law, and the few became much fewer. Just about everyone who wasn't already connected became so because there was no choice; the few radicals who broke the law were quickly rounded up and connected anyway. Escape was practically impossible; as you can imagine, anyone not connected is instantly identifiable, and anyway, where could you escape to?"

Occasionally they passed a person walking the other way on the path, invariably wearing a wide-brimmed hat dripping with rain. Lennox greeted each one cheerily in English or French or German, and each one stared up at Tommy as if he had two heads. "We make most of our own supplies; other stuff, hardware, electrical items, guns, we get from abandoned cities and towns. We make do pretty well, given our circumstances." They came across a pen where a few pigs were lying under a shelter. "That's Roger," Lennox said, shaking his head and smiling. "He wanted to have pigs, so we brought some pigs. There are some alpaca in the open fields, sheep, goats, even cows and bulls. We have a few small vegetable gardens at the edge of the forest where there is more light, but they have to be small so that they don't give away our presence."

"How many of you are there?"

"Freemen? By some estimates there are about 2 000 left in the Central Europe Fallowlands. Whether there are others elsewhere on the planet, I don't know. There used to be, that's a fact; but now: who knows? There's no way for us to communicate. And there's certainly no way for a Freeman to travel very far without being identified, immediately captured, and then linked to the Mother. So we are completely cut off from any of our brethren on any other continent. But I have to believe that Freemen still live in hidden pockets in Africa, Australia, North America . . ."

"Where are they all? Two thousand? I've seen a total of about 15."

"There are little enclaves of 50 or 100 here and there, hidden away. Keep in mind that the Fallowlands encompass almost a half a million square kilometres. Where are they? I know where a half-dozen of them are found, and that's more than almost anyone else. We don't talk much about where we are; if someone is captured by the Hive, then the Mother knows what he knows. There's one a day's walk or so from here; that's where most of our food really comes from."

"This isn't an 'enclave'?"

"I would call this more an 'outpost.'"

"An outpost for what?"

Lennox shrugged. "Just an outpost."

They walked in silence for a time. The terrain was complex and the path, which Tommy found barely discernable, weaved through in such a manner that he could rarely anticipate where it led nor look back and definitively see where he'd been. There was an occasional descent, but for the most part, they were gaining elevation. After his month of confinement, the exertion felt good, even with the rain. And his senses were particularly keen, as though they had been pared with a blade. Such a change from the last time he had been taken away from the camp! What had happened to his eyes? The colours around him were rich despite the grey, dull light. It was like he was seeing, really *seeing*, the forest for the first time. Had it always been like this? Forest: growth and decay in equal parts. Green moss softly cloaked a fallen tree like fur. Here beside a dark hollow log was a plant with red berries, there by a root a drooping purple flower, bouncing as it was smacked with a large drop of water fallen from overhead. A dead tree was pockmarked with holes drilled by woodpeckers. Mushrooms popped from the ground in colours of white or yellow. The moist air was thick with rich, fungal scent. He could almost taste it. And steady was the rain with a sound like the sea.

"Do you understand why we have been forced to keep you under guard, Tommy? If you had escaped, if you'd made it back to your people, you'd be reconnected, your knowledge of our presence and location would be available to your authorities, and we would have to move on or be captured. Certainly, you see that. That was our automatic fear when you first found us, accidental as it was: that we'd been discovered. With no reason to suspect that there was a glitch in your connection, there was no choice but to kill you and de-camp – move on to some new hiding place. But then we realized that you *hadn't* been connected – the back of your head was cool – what luck! We could have, of course, just killed you, and everything would have continued as it was, but, no, what an opportunity! An opportunity to free someone from the Mother."

"Well, dammit, I didn't want to be freed. If you were acting out of such . . . such . . . sanctimonious generosity, don't you think you should have asked *me* what *I* want?"

"Just a sidebar for a moment, Tommy: 'sanctimonious generosity'? I'm impressed with the improvement in your ability to express yourself. You've come a long way from 'piss off.' But to your question: no, of course, we shouldn't have asked you. No one who is linked to the Mother is going to agree to be disconnected. When you were in your mother's womb – of course, I don't know if your mother opted for a natural birth or whether you were incubated, but let's not quibble over the metaphor – when you were in your mother's womb, if somebody had asked you if you wanted to stay put or be pulled into some unknown universe, what would you have answered?"

"Well, if I'm comparing my universe to your universe, I can tell you which one is desirable and which one is lacking . . ."

"Which one, Tommy? Which is the desirable one?"

"Are they even close? In mine, at least my *former* one, I have the knowledge of the world, the whole world, closer than my fingertips. I can talk to my girlfriends anytime, anywhere, like *that!*" – he snapped his fingers. "I can find out what's happening in Japan and the price of watermelons at the store while I'm watching Wimbledon tennis and Tour de France at the same time . . . In your universe, you're huddled in tents, reading books with no images and no sound, leading purposeless lives, without access to the great things that are happening in the world, you can't even communicate without meeting face to face – you're like cavemen!"

"I suppose much of that is true, although 'purposeless lives' seems a little harsh, and I'd hazard that we're somewhat beyond living like cavemen. Nevertheless, you're neglecting a key point: we're free. Free to ponder what we want. Free to make our own images when we read a book. Free to have silence. Free to listen to the rain for no reason, without a million voices in our heads. Most of all, free to think without our thoughts being overheard. That's the main one, Tommy, that's the key one: our thoughts, our actions, they're our own. Nobody eavesdrops. Privacy. It's priceless."

"Ah . . ." Tommy waved his hand dismissively. "Privacy's of no relevance unless you're thinking something contemptible or subversive or doing something illegal. In which case, being overheard is a good thing for everybody. But if your head's above water and your nose is clean, who cares if somebody knows what you're thinking or doing?"

"Do you really believe that? It's not right, Tommy. It's not right that everybody knows what you are thinking and what you are doing all the time. And it was never like that, not before T-Day. Then . . . privacy disappeared in such tiny increments that nobody realized what they were losing. And when it was all gone, people wondered what was so important about it in the first place."

"T-Day . . . ?"

"Oh, never mind. A day of infamy in the history of the world, as related by the Freemen. I'll explain it someday. For now, it's not important; I don't want you to miss the point. The point is this: we've cut you free, Tommy. For the first time since you were connected, you are free. I know it's been tough; you've been weaned rather forcefully. It's a pain that I never experienced. But I think you are ready now to appreciate what freedom from the Mother really means."

"I like your idea of freedom: confine me to a tent and post a guard with a rifle."

"There's no guard now, as you doubtless noticed. You're free to go, if you want. I can even show you the way back, to find your people."

Tommy stopped instantly. Was he serious? He could go? It was finished?

"You'll . . . you'll show me how to go?"

Lennox nodded.

"All right." *Home. I can get home! I can be reconnected!* Still, he hesitated. *Why? Why am I hesitating?* It would be so good to just get the hell out of there, get back home, get reconnected to the Hive . . .

He tried to laugh lightly, but it came out sounding strained. "I think there will be some pretty upset people waiting for you when you get back."

"They've been upset with me before. In time, they'll understand. This has to be your choice, not anybody else's."

"You can't be serious. You really think that I would even consider staying here? In a backwoods forest with a hopeless group of semi-savages? Look what I have back home! How can you compare real society to this? Besides: I have my career, my family, my friends, my contacts . . ."

"The Mother . . ."

"Yes! Everything the Hive has to offer!" What decision needed to be made? Wasn't his course of action obvious? "If I go, you will have to pull up camp and move somewhere else."

"True . . ."

Another pause. *So what? They've done it before, they can do it again . . .* "You don't know what I'm thinking, do you. You're gambling."

"A little."

"Shit." Tommy turned and walked a few steps along the trail. "Shit, shit, shit, shit, SHIT LA MERDE!" He turned again. His mind was seething, a pit of snakes. "I don't know what to think. I'm . . . I'm . . ." He hadn't seen the blitzing linebacker. *To be back, home, reconnected, my friends, my contacts, Luker, the Hive . . . YES! But . . . but do I really want that? Do I want those people in my head again? Do I want to give up my silence?*

He was walking back and forth, 5 metres this way, 5 that way. *Why am I even hesitating? Here's the chance I've been waiting for! Am I an idiot? Of course, I want to be home, to be out of this nightmare! Let's go!* But his feet wouldn't take him anywhere. He realized that this is what he had been struggling with in his dreamless sleeps – a confrontation of his two worlds. Which world was right? He needed to make a decision; in his former life, the only decision he had to make was which receiver to throw the ball to.

His head was pounding. The ground beneath him seemed to have lost its firmness. He was overwhelmed with the weight, the significance, of Lennox's offer. *I'm so alone here . . .* "SHIT!" he shouted again. "You'll really show me how to get back to civilization?"

Lennox nodded.

Tommy turned, came back again, arms waving wildly. *"What happens to the rabbits? In the story! I want to know what happens to the rabbits!"* His face was twisted in agony.

Finally, he screamed into Lennox's face, "I DON'T KNOW WHAT I WANT!"

The rain swallowed the sound, like sand scattered onto a lake.

"Yes, you do, Tommy," Lennox said quietly. "You do."

"My head is splitting."

"I know." Lennox reached up and put his hand on Tommy's shoulder. "You've had enough time in the rain. Let's head back."

◊

Tommy walked into the 'mess tent' for his first meal there, and conversations among the six or seven men present stopped instantly. At least two of them Tommy recognized as having guarded him at one time or another. Every eye was on him. The men were seated at one of two long tables, each about 5 metres in length and running along the sides of the tent, with enough space between them for two people to walk abreast. At the end of the tent, opposite from where Tommy had entered, there was a serving table, with three large steaming pots along with stacks of wooden dishes and cups and an assortment of other food-related items that he didn't classify with his first glance. A man armed with a ladle stood behind the table, his gaze also fixed upon the newcomer.

Ten enormous seconds went by as Tommy stood there, not sure whether he should move forward or backward, before a young blond-haired man of about 19 said to him, "Pick up a plate and get some food." At that instant, Lennox entered, beating the rain from his jacket with his hands. He slapped Tommy on the back with his hand while he said something briefly to the others in German. They responded incoherently with what Tommy perceived as a somewhat unenthusiastic greeting. He raised his hand and shyly said, "Hello."

He followed Lennox to the table at the far end and, following the other's example, picked up a tray from underneath and placed plate, bowl, cup, and utensils on it. The man behind the counter slopped a creamy soup into the bowl and placed a piece of meat and a scoop of a soggy vegetable mixture on his plate.

"*Il va manger beaucoup plus que ça, Jacques!*" Lennox said to the man behind the table, and a second piece and a second scoop were added to Tommy's plate. The two of them then poured water into their cups from a jug, and they sat down facing each other at one end of the unoccupied long table.

"How are you as a cook?"

Tommy shook his head as he forked a piece of meat into his mouth. "Never done it."

"So I guess you won't be adding to our culinary repertoire. Too bad. Food gets a bit tedious around here. At any rate, you'll be cooking for us at some point; everybody takes a turn. Don't worry; you'll be with somebody experienced. Tonight, you are going to wash dishes, though. No experience necessary. That's something else that everybody takes turns at. Just so happens that tonight is your turn."

"Does everybody eat here? In this tent?"

Lennox moved his head ambiguously. "Most people do, most of the time. Morning and evening meals are always available here; some people prefer to do their own."

"What kind of meat is this?" Tommy found the food particularly tasty, then realized it was probably because it was significantly warmer than the tray-delivered food he was accustomed to receiving in the tent.

"Alpaca."

Tommy was about to respond when a woman, perhaps in her mid-twenties, entered, brushing the rain from her jacket. She emitted a startled, "Oh!" when she saw Tommy. The men at the other table laughed.

"Tina, you haven't met Tommy Antikagamac yet," Lennox said, turning to face the newcomer.

"No, uh, hello," she said uncertainly with an unidentifiable accent, and then she went to get her tray.

A few moments later, two others entered: one was Ameline, and with her was the man who had shot at Tommy in the woods.

"Bonjour," Ameline said to Lennox and Tommy. She was clearly surprised to see the latter, but she chose not to make any special acknowledgement of his presence. If she was happy to see him, Tommy couldn't tell.

The other simply nodded in Tommy's direction, without saying anything.

"Harrison is an interesting man," Lennox said when the two newcomers had gone to the serving table. "American. At least, his parents were American, but living in Europe when they were forced underground. He's as prickly as a porcupine, but he loves birds. You should see some of his sketches. Oh, yes, he's quite an artist. And you'd never know it to listen to him, but he's very religious. Do you believe in God, Tommy?

"Of course not."

"That came out quite flippantly. Is that the general feeling among the people of the Hive?"

"Pretty much. At any rate, it's illegal."

"Illegal? Illegal to believe in God? Your Hive seems very restrictive, Tommy. Do they actually police your minds? How can you make a belief illegal?"

"No, no, you've got it wrong. It's just the *opposite* of restrictive. We're free, completely free, to think whatever we want, believe anything we want. It's *religion* that imposes restrictions on people's thoughts. We've moved beyond that. And we've moved beyond the conflicts, the wars, the bloodshed that religion has caused. We're free from all that. It's over. We've cured ourselves."

"So you can believe anything you want, as long as you don't believe in God."

"Well, I suppose you *can* believe in God, just like you can believe in Santa Claus or the Tooth Fairy. As long as it's just in your own head. But what's illegal is to *eegress* thoughts to try to convince people about God or religion or anything like that, and it's illegal to manifest religion in any way. And that's made the world a much nicer place. So let me correct myself. You *can* believe in God . . ."

"As long as you don't tell anybody or think about it . . ."

"Well, yeah, as long as you don't push your religion on anybody. It's *religion* that's illegal."

"I see."

At that moment, Ameline and Harrison sat with their trays at the opposite end of the table at which Lennox and Tommy were eating. Tommy took the opportunity to look down at his food and begin eating more earnestly. He was hungry, and the conversation with Lennox had made him uncomfortable, as conversations with Lennox often did.

Later, as the people at the other table began to get up and leave, two of them came up to Tommy.

"Monsieur Antikagamac," a short, stocky man with a balding head and a black moustache began with a French accent, "my young friend 'ere wanted to meet you but 'e was too shy to come 'imself." The young friend, on whose shoulder the stocky man had his hand, was the blond fellow who had invited Tommy to pick up a plate when he had first entered the tent.

"I'm not shy," the young man said, embarrassed.

Tommy put his fork down and put his hand out. "It's a pleasure to meet you . . ."

"Myles, sir. Myles Weiskopf." His hand was engulfed by Tommy's enormous paw. "I've been watching you since you came to London."

"You can call me Tommy." A fan. If there was one thing Tommy was accustomed to, it was the fawning of fans.

"Myles is a big fan of American football," Lennox said. "To be honest, Tommy, he's the *only* fan among the Freemen that I'm aware of. He plays around with our computer when it's not being used, and decodes the satellite feed from the games."

"I can only get the European games," Myles said.

"The European Conference is the best," Tommy replied.

"Why h'are you called TeePee?" the stocky man asked.

"My name's Tommy Pierre. T. P. And I'm a quarter Native North American. My grandfather was a Quebec Algonquin. So I guess it was natural that they would start calling me TeePee."

"So you from America?"

"Originally from Quebec City. Canada. That's where I started in football. I only went to Chicago when I was drafted there. And of course, then I was traded to London."

"Biggest mistake Chicago ever made," Myles piped in.

Tommy smiled.

"Tommy Pierre Antikagamac," Lennox said. "I always thought that was an odd combination of names."

"My grandfather married a French Canadian. My grandmother on my mother's side was of Irish descent. She married an Italian, believe it or not."

"Your parents, dey must have been 'uge," the stocky man said.

"All he knows of his blood parents are their registration numbers," Ameline said from the end of the table. Tommy had glanced in her direction several times while he had been eating, but she had never looked away from her meal.

"My father was about your height," he said to Myles, ignoring Ameline. "And my mother was about yours," he said with a smirk to the stocky man.

"It's hard to imagine anyone ever tackling you," Myles said. "You're so big."

"Well, a lot of those defensive guys are a whole lot bigger. Believe me."

A tall man, who had started to leave but had come back, said something in German to the stocky man. "'Ow many kilos can you lift over your 'ead?" the stocky man translated.

"Oh, about 150, 160."

"*Sacre bleu!*" somebody said.

A rain-soaked man who had just entered the tent joined the group around Tommy, as did Tina. "What's de biggest person you play wit?" the stocky man asked.

"Hah!" Tommy laughed. "Milky Johnson, Chicago Bears' tackle, is six eleven and 505 pounds."

"Two metres ten, 230 kilos," someone converted.

The crowd around Tommy, which now numbered six or seven, buzzed with incredulity.

"But that's unusual. Most offensive linemen are 400, 450, and they are the biggest players on the team. There are all kinds of different sizes with different positions. There's one receiver I play with who's only a 198."

"People don't get that big naturally," someone said. "You all must eat growth hormones and steroids and all that crap."

"Not at all. The league has very strict rules concerning biochemical substances and implants . . ."

"I'm sure there are ways to get around the rules."

Tommy laughed again. "You forget: in the Hive, there is no 'getting around the rules.' In the Hive, you can't cheat. You can't lie. It never even occurs to you."

"Were you always big?" – this from Tina – "I can't picture you as a child. How did your mother feed you?"

"I was a big child, no question. But I was with a football program from the time I was seven. They took care of feeding me."

There were a couple of questions about the game of American football itself; most of them seemed to have only a very vague idea about how the sport was played.

"TeePee was the Super Bowl MVP last year," Myles pointed out. "He threw three touchdown passes and ran for 87 yards." His familiarity with the game, and with Tommy, was allowing him to claim a certain status within this group. Just like a typical fan, Tommy mused mildly.

"What's it like to play in front of eighty-thousand people?" Myles asked.

The question caught Tommy off guard, and he didn't answer right away. He couldn't answer. *What's it like?* That's a question you never had to answer in the Hive; if someone wanted to know "what's it like," they just ingressed your thoughts. Eighty-thousand people: the capacity of King William Stadium. A drop in a bucket. It

67

wasn't the 80 000 people in the stands that weighed on his mind; it was the hundred million who were watching him on jennix, those new 3-D sensurworld screens. It was the hundreds of thousands of people ingressing his thoughts pre-game, at half time, after he threw a touchdown pass, after he threw an interception. *What's it like?*

"It's exciting," he finally said.

*

"Is Felix your son?" Tommy asked. He and Frenna were on their way to the latter's tent in order to choose a second book for him to read.

Frenna stopped abruptly. "How . . .?" she started, but then relaxed and continued walking. "The inscription. Of course. I'd forgotten. Yes. He was learning English. That was his first English book."

"Where does he live now? Is he here in this camp?"

"No. No, I'm afraid Felix died quite some time ago."

Tommy was startled. "I . . . I'm sorry to hear that. What happened to him?"

"Sickness. It happens. He just became ill with something, and within a couple of weeks, he died."

"I'm really sorry . . ."

"It was a long time ago. Here's my tent." Tommy didn't push the issue.

Frenna's tent was almost identical to Tommy's in shape and size. As Tommy saw when he stepped inside, that's where the similarity ended. His was utilitarian; Frenna's actually had decorations. Hanging from an overhead cross-support was some sort of display about the size of a football, made up of feathers and dried grasses and flowers. At eye level along one side of the tent were half a dozen brightly coloured drawings of birds; Tommy wondered if the artist was Harrison. In a corner was a small table holding nothing but a vase with flowers and three odd-shaped rocks. Most impressive, however, was the item that made Tommy's jaw drop as soon as he stepped in: a multi-levelled shelf supporting what must have been almost a hundred authentic word-printed-on-paper-books. All totally illegal, of course. Thrilling enough to make the hairs on his forearms stand up.

"Wow!" Tommy muttered.

"I thought you would like it. Back home, I mean, the larger community where my main home is, I have many more books. It wasn't easy to bring this collection way out here, but I have to have books with me. They're a testament to where we've come from."

Tommy sensed that the "where we've come from" encompassed something significantly more substantial than her home community, whatever that was.

"You know that your people destroy books." She said it the same way one might say, 'You know that your people squish rare butterflies.'

"Just paper-books. But everything's in regular books anyway."

"Those aren't books. You know now that they aren't. Books, real books with *words, these* books, don't limit your thoughts by showing you what to see. Real books allow your mind to soar, to flee space, to be free. Haven't you noticed that books are warm? Feel the pages. They're warm to the touch. That's because they have life. Real books are alive."

A month ago, he would have dismissed that idea with a flip of his hand. Now . . . he wasn't so sure. He found himself staring at the bookshelf, mesmerized. Titles in French and German and English.

"You said you liked science fiction." Frenna pulled out a book. "You might like this."

Tommy read the title, with a touch of difficulty: "*The Martian Chronicles*." Ray Bradbury. He opened it up, flipped through some of the pages. "Do you . . . do you have any other books with animals?"

"Animals. Ummm . . . yes. Yes, I think I know just what you want." Frenna examined the shelves for a few moments. "Give me a moment . . . Ah! Here we go." She removed a second book and gave it to Tommy, taking *The Martian Chronicles* from his hands and replacing it in the bookshelf.

"*The Call of the Wild*," Tommy read aloud slowly.

"Do you like dogs?"

"I don't know. I mean, I don't mind them, but I've never had one. Never really thought about it."

"I've seen you watching birds and chipmunks. I think you're an animal lover at heart. Anyway, I'm sure you'll like this book."

Tommy nodded thoughtfully. "Thanks," he said. Then, "Frenna, what *is* this place?"

Frenna laughed. "What, my tent?"

"No." Tommy gestured vaguely with his hands. "This . . . place. This . . . camp. These tents. You. Lennox. Ameline. What are you doing here? This isn't your home. So what are all of you doing here?"

"We have to explore, Tommy. To find places where we can live. We have to always be ready to move somewhere, to abandon a village and find another place in an instant. We're never safe. That's the life we live as Freemen. All it takes is one member of the Hive to stumble upon us, as you did, and send an image and a geo-location to the Mother, and we have to move, find somewhere else to hide. There are many outposts like this, feeling the land like tentacles."

Tommy shook his head. "No. No, there's more, isn't there? I mean, I'm sure there's truth to what you say, but there's part of the story that's missing. Lennox tells me the same thing you do, but things don't add up. You don't act like a bunch of explorers."

"And how should explorers act?"

"I don't know. A group of you will be talking, but as soon as I come near, everybody stops and looks at me as if they don't want me to hear what they are saying. As if I could understand anyway . . ."

"Well, isn't that to be expected? You're a giant, an outsider, a member of the Hive. People don't know how to take you."

"I think it's more than that. Look, this is all new, where everybody's thoughts are hidden from me. It's frustrating as hell, believe me. But somehow, and I can't explain how, but I sense that it's not just that your thoughts are inaccessible; it's that you are actually *hiding* your thoughts. You are telling me things so as to mislead me."

Frenna smiled. "Imagination, Tommy. Your mind is learning to use its imagination, and that's a good thing. It's a sign of progress. Sometimes I imagine that a squirrel is talking to me, and I try to understand what its chattering really means. Sometimes I try to imagine what it would be like to live in a city or to live in another time. But as for this place, don't worry. No one is misleading you. Things are as I've said.

"Use your imagination for other things."

Tommy made a conscious effort to push aside his misgivings, and moved on to other topics. He enjoyed talking with Frenna, enjoyed just *being* with her really, although he wasn't quite sure why. He hardly knew her. They had nothing in common. She was nowhere close to his age. He suppressed a laugh. Why with her, of all people, should he have this connection?

He spent an hour in her tent, talking about her favourite books, meteor showers (he'd never seen one with his own eyes), wolves, winter. When he left, the sun had already drifted below the level of the mountains to the west so that, even though he could see blue sky through gaps in the overhead trees, the camp had become embraced by evening shadow. He was looking forward to an evening meal, and then an hour reading his book under the electric light in his tent. If Frenna said he would like it, then he was sure that he would.

But why would she be lying about the purpose of this camp?

*

Tommy woke up in a sweat. It had been a very disturbing dream, but it vanished even as he tried to remember it, like mist that you try to grab hold of. All he remembered was hands, thousands of them all over him, and then even that memory was gone.

7

About a half kilometre southwest of the camp, the forest gave way to an open clearing of knee-high grass and wild yellow flowers. The slope here was gentle, unthreatening even to an acrophobic like Tommy. A herd of 20 or 30 alpaca would frequently be seen grazing leisurely. These were a source of milk, and occasionally meat, for the small Freeman outpost. Because of the exposure to the open sky, however, the Freemen generally avoided the area, other than for limited forays in early morning or late evening.

It was near midnight, and the sky was black as ink. Stars blazed brilliantly. Tommy stared at patterns that, millennia earlier, ancients had organized into constellations. With mixed feelings, he contemplated the fact that the only one he recognized was the Great Dipper, hovering low, just over the mountains to the north. High in the sky was a W; he knew that was something, but he couldn't remember what. Other groups he knew were creatures or gods or heroes, bright stars had names, ghostly puffs were clusters of stars or distant galaxies, and with Skywatch he could identify them all. Now nothing, save the Great Dipper.

He, like most of humanity, rarely saw the night sky black like this; city lights made the slivers of sky between high-rising buildings an anemic milky-purple paste, uninspiring as wastewater. But here, in the Fallowlands! My goodness, the immensity of the heavenly vault! Grains of sugar sprinkled on a black velvet train. The Milky Way (Ah! he remembered *that* name!) like a pale river meandering with celestial purpose.

He lay on his back, staring at the sky. Alone. Alone in the middle of the clearing, tall grass all around him, the chirping of a thousand crickets playing a symphony in his ears.

Alone in his head.

It occurred to him that the last time he had looked at the night sky like this was just over a year ago. The Australian Fallowlands that time. Another retreat from the public eye, if not the public mind, his ceeb status getting him access to places off-limits to everyone else.

And he'd stared at the dark night sky then, too. But not like this. He had Skywatch and a half-dozen astronomers showing him things. Wonderful things. Exciting things. And as he thrilled to his discoveries in the night sky, he would eegress his thoughts, his emotions, his *feelings*, to his 3 000 contacts. Constantly. It would never have occurred to him to contain his impassioned thoughts within his own mind, even had it been possible. He felt a need to share them with others as keen as hunger. Meanwhile, hundreds of people were sharing and comparing their *own* visions and thoughts and experiences with *him*, and of these, he was allowing a dozen or so access to his conscious mind. And of course, he was aware of countless thousands and thousands of people all over the world ingressing his thoughts. As a ceeb, he'd grown quite accustomed to that.

He shuddered now as he thought back to that time, those feelings. It was like his head had been full of ants. The noise, the constant noise. Now it was quiet. He looked at the sky, knowing nothing except the Great Dipper and the Milky Way, and felt a thrill more keen, more *profound*, than anything he had experienced before.

He was alone!

Alone, and silently crying.

And he didn't know if he was crying because he was joyful, or because he was sadder than he had ever been in his life. In the confusion that was his mind, he couldn't tell the difference. He was hoping the stars would answer him.

A week ago, he was sleeping 14 hours a night. Now, he was having trouble sleeping at all. Lennox told him not to worry; his brain was still adapting. Tonight, he had left when the camp was quiet, walking slowly and carefully along a trail that, when he turned off his flashlight, was black as pitch. He was unnerved, scared even, at the nighttime unfamiliarity of the trail, but he'd moved on anyway. He felt compelled. And when the trail passed from the woods into the clearing, and the star-drenched sky opened up with its dazzling brilliance, it was like he had been underwater and had just broken the surface. And now he was lying on his back, staring at the stars with tears in his eyes.

He wondered again whether or not the break from the Hive had rendered him insane.

A bright star appeared above the northwest horizon, brighter than all the other stars, arcing slowly across the sky. *Spacecruzer 1*. Or *2*, or *3*. Crew of 25, with 150 passengers, each paying a unicorn's testicle to be able to orbit the Earth for a week. The star moved across the northern sky, winking out of sight behind unseen mountains to the east after a minute or two. Other moving stars, much fainter ones, also moved silently against the celestial backdrop, perhaps a dozen in view at any particular time. A sky made busy to serve the Mother. He looked at the satellites with distaste.

In fact, everything that had to do with the Hive gave him a sick feeling in the pit of his stomach. He couldn't even think of his contacts, his family, his teammates . . . nothing, without feeling twisted inside. Had all his relationships been so shallow that they meant nothing when they were severed? Was the feeling in his stomach there because he had come to truly resent the whole concept of the Hive and it made him sick, or was it because deep inside, he felt guilty of somehow being a traitor?

He was so confused. His brain was something adrift, lost in the silent space between the stars. He was neither there nor here.

The stars staring at him with eternal majesty and lofty indifference. The satellites between them in their frenetic silence.

He must have fallen asleep because there were fewer stars overhead. The unnamed constellations had shifted, pinwheeling counter-clockwise about the Pole Star. He sat up. The sky behind the stars was a deep, dark blue, and towards the east, the mountains were silhouetted against a vaguely crimson horizon.

"It's the colour of blood," he said quietly. He stood up.

"Hey," he shouted to the stars, "the sky's bleeding!" He laughed strangely, then spun around in a circle. He bared his teeth and made a hissing sound. He curled his fingers and swiped his hand viciously through the air in front of him.

"The great cat scratched the eyeball of the sky!" he exclaimed dramatically. "And dawn bled." He laughed again, then put his hands to the side of his head. His headache was back. He lay back down and squinted his eyes closed. From the woods, he heard the rich-throated song of a robin. A vision of a dozen robins in the trees came to his head, then a hundred of them, then a thousand, then the trees laden with tens of thousands of robins, crowding every branch, and he was asleep.

He awakened with the morning sun in his eyes, already well above the mountains to the east.

His headache was gone.

*

It had taken over a month for him to struggle his way through his first paper-book; the second took him two weeks. He was now on his third: *Treasure Island.*

And the turmoil in his mind had quieted. The revolution was complete.

No longer was he questioning his decision not to leave the Freemen. He did not want to be back in the city, did not want to be a ceeb, did not want the shallowness of his "contacts," and definitely did not want people in his head. No, when he thought of the Hive now, it was no longer with the sick feeling he'd been experiencing; it was with pure, simple disgust. To give up his privacy, the sanctity of his thoughts, to relinquish his newly discovered individuality to the consuming collectivity of the Hive! The thought had become execrable. Never again.

He hated the Mother.

And he marvelled at that realization. How could he have so utterly changed his attitude, rejecting his whole charmed life and the utopia of established society to embrace this primitive anti-social blight, these *Ketchen*, in such a short time? It really was quite likely that he *was* insane. And perhaps the fact that he no longer cared whether or not he was insane was further evidence that he was indeed so.

"I'm not the one to comment on your sanity," Harrison said. "Your turn." He handed Tommy the shovel he'd been using; the two of them were taking turns digging a new latrine. Harrison took a long drink from a canteen of water. "I hate to admit it, but Lennox was right about you. You're acting exactly as he predicted. Which means I have to apologize for calling him a fucking asshole. Not that he isn't, but he was right about you."

"What do you mean, 'I'm like he predicted'?"

"Just what I said." Harrison sat on a stump. He had his shirt off, as did Tommy. Harrison was well-muscled, and in regular company would be considered a large man, but next to Tommy, he looked tiny. "Me, I figured, 'Once a Hive-boy, always a Hive-boy.' I saw three possible things happening to you. Thing number one, nothing. You'd just stay like you were, pacing your tent, waiting for a chance to escape. Month after month. Eventually, we'd give up and have to shoot you. Thing number two, you'd become a raging psychopath. You'd go berserk or something, and we'd have to shoot you. Then there's thing number three, that's where you lose your marbles and become a blubbering baby, slobbering and crying and sucking your thumb, and we'd have to shoot you to put you out of your misery."

"But Lennox?"

"Hey, that hole's not gonna dig itself, you know. Thing in your hand's called a shovel. Lennox, he had a certain intuition. He likes to call it psychoanalysis, but I think he just took a guess and got lucky. He said your brain was being shocked, sure as if it was being struck by a bolt of lightning. You were part of the Hive, and then instantly you are out, ripped away from it, not just ripped away but instantly immersed into a different world, where your free-falling brain grabs hold of anything it can, and the only thing of substance it can hold onto is the exact opposite of what it knew. It wasn't just, 'Hmmm . . . Hive, hmmm . . . Freemen . . . I'll compare and make a choice.' It was, like I said, more like a shock.

Lennox said that you'd end up more a Freeman than any of us. But of course, you're the only one in the world this has ever happened to, the only person who's ever left the Hive, so he was just guessing. He said you'd either turn completely anti-Hive, or you'd become a blubbering, slobbering idiot. In which case, we'd have to shoot you."

Tommy dug in silence for a time. "You talk a lot about shooting. Do you shoot people often? Is that something I can expect if I stay here?" His mood had become rather melancholy.

"We'll shoot people if we have to. It's a matter of survival, and we'll do what we need to survive." Harrison was quiet for a few moments, then continued. "You know, Tommy-boy," he continued, "fact is I've never shot anybody. Never even shot an animal. Good thing for you; I suppose if I'd had a bit more practice, you wouldn't be alive right now. And I'd be digging that hole all by my lonesome."

"You sound regretful."

Harrison didn't respond right away. "You might have been the end of us, you know. You find us, you send our location to the Mother, the Hive comes with their fucking air transports, they round us up, and we all end up in hell. I needed to shoot you, but I couldn't put the aiming and the trigger-pulling together. It's like something wouldn't let me."

"Too bad."

"You know, when I think about it, you're so fucking lucky! Pretty well everyone here's a better shot than me. Hans, Karl, Frenna, hell, even Lennox! Anybody else spots you and . . ."

"Frenna? I hardly think Frenna would be dangerous with a gun."

"You kidding? Frenna's the best shot here. The best. It's in her blood. Her grandfather was a prize-winning marksman, back

79

when the world was a different place. I've seen her take down a deer from 200 metres. Incredible."

"Are we talking about the same person? I'm talking about the little woman, fifty-ish, greying hair . . . likes books . . . I can't even imagine her with a gun."

"Probably good to keep it that way. Wait! Sshhh!"

"What?"

"*Sshhh!*"

Tommy was instantly alert. He was dispirited and tired, and all this talk about shooting intruders had him on edge. He was waist-deep in the hole they had been digging and he held himself frozen, listening. He heard nothing but a light breeze gently drawing breath through the upper branches high above. Harrison was standing now, quite still. He lifted a hand very slowly, and pointed to something beyond Tommy's left shoulder.

"There," he said quietly.

Tommy carefully turned to the direction to which Harrison was pointing. He saw nothing.

"That big mother of a pine. Ten metres up, just above the second branch."

Tommy saw a streak of yellow as the bird flew off deeper into the woods.

"Golden oriole," Harrison said. "Beautiful bird."

"You know birds?"

"I love birds. Watched 'em since I was a kid. I keep a notebook. Over the years, I've logged sightings of 63 different kinds. Sixty-three. Any given day, I can identify a dozen just by their songs."

Tommy had been on a field trip to an American bird sanctuary area a few years earlier. In just one day and with no experience, he had seen and identified 38 different species, a dozen of which were quite exotic. But of course, BirdPro had done most of the work for him.

"'Watching birds' doesn't fit with someone who's disappointed he wasn't able to shoot and kill me."

"Life is complex, isn't it?"

Tommy climbed out of the hole and handed the shovel to Harrison, then took a drink from the canteen and sat on the stump.

"Lennox says that you're religious."

"Lennox thinks he's got everybody here figured out." Harrison dropped himself into the hole and began shovelling.

"Are you?"

"What, religious? No, I wouldn't say particularly. Four or five of us get together on Sundays and say a prayer."

"That sounds religious. What do you say? I'm curious; I've never heard a prayer."

"'*Thanks the Lord, we're here alive;*

Keep us from the fucking Hive.'"

"That's a prayer?"

"There are various renditions, but that's the gist."

"I expected something more formal."

"I wash myself in the morning. Did you know that my grand-mother was a Catholic? Before the Hive? Secretly, of course, because Catholics, the few that were left, were typically whipped in public if they were found out. My uncle betrayed her. She died in prison."

"Subversion is in your blood."

"Freedom is in my blood."

There was a leather pack with some provisions at the base of a nearby tree; Tommy went and helped himself to a biscuit. "Want one?"

"Sure," Harrison answered. "Give me the canteen too."

The two men took a break, the only sound coming from the crunching of the biscuits and the whispering of the breeze.

"What is 'T-Day'?"

Harrison cocked his head. "Now where did a Hive-boy like you hear about T-Day?"

"Lennox mentioned it."

"I see. Well, T-Day is not so easy to explain because there's no real exact meaning, if you know what I mean. *T* can stand for a lot of things – technology, tyranny, transition, travesty, tragedy – but I'd say most people think that it comes from the word 'transistor.' That is, the darkest day in the history of humanity, seen from the perspective of someone looking back from the end of time, is the invention of the transistor. It's not as simple as that, of course; but we look at that as a kind of tipping point. There's before, and there's after."

"I don't understand."

"Then don't interrupt. Where did the Hive come from? What's the seed from which it was born? People look at the invention of the transistor 137 years ago as the point where technology took over the reins of our civilization from our feeble hands. No transistor means no internet, which means no skin electronics, which means no implants, which means no cortical connections, which means no Hive. Of course, like I said, it's just a symbol; when you walk into a blind race run by blind people, how can you tell where they started from? Some people say the *T* should stand for telephone, and say *that*'s where the tipping point occurred. It doesn't matter. We vilify the names of Bardeen and Brattain and Shockley, but of course, if they hadn't been around, if the transistor hadn't been invented in nineteen forty fucking seven or whenever, somebody else would have invented it in forty fucking nine. But people like their symbols, so that's why we have T-Day. It's stupid, but it's important for some people, so I let them have their peace every October 12."

"Why October 12?"

"Fucked if I know. As good a date as any, I guess."

Harrison went back to digging.

"Nobody's ever said so to me, but I take it that Lennox is in charge here, no?" Tommy asked.

"Ah! Nobody's really in charge. Lennox probably thinks he is. He's the oldest. He says a lot of things; people usually ignore him. But things here pretty well run themselves. We don't need anybody 'in charge.'"

"I take it you're not Lennox's biggest fan."

"No, no, don't get the wrong idea. Lennox is a good man, and we get along fine. Everybody here is fine. I talk about everybody the same way."

"But Lennox is the doctor?"

"Naw, he's not a doctor, any more than any of us. We've all learned how to care for ourselves. I guess maybe he knows the most. He has more experience than anybody else here, and he's probably studied it more, so, yeah, I guess you could say he's 'the doctor.' But, really, we all know basic stuff, and if a problem is more complicated than wrapping a wound, we all put our heads together."

"You must get sicknesses here? Diseases? Contagious stuff? In the Hive, we're monitored every 8 hours, and antibiotics are updated daily as new strains of bacteria are identified. There is no contagious disease in the Hive. But here? People must get sick . . . How do you treat people when they get sick?"

"People don't get sick here much. We're pretty hygienic, and we're pretty hardy. People get colds; big deal. If someone gets sick, they get sick. We deal with it the best we can."

"When Frenna's boy got sick, was that here? Or was he in an enclave?"

Harrison stopped shovelling. "Frenna's boy?"

"Felix. I heard he died from an illness of some sort."

Harrison went back to his work. "Lennox must have told you that."

"No, Frenna."

Harrison continued to dig without answering. A minute went by, awkwardly, and Tommy decided that this was a line of questioning he wouldn't pursue now. He'd clearly struck a nerve; perhaps he'd ask Lennox about it later.

"Felix was a good kid," Harrison finally said, digging harder. "He loved stars. He loved birds. Loved to draw them. Then the fuckers came. Two helis. Must have been 30 of them, with their black bullet-proof suits and their blasters . . . All that, and they just took three of us. Everyone was running, but they didn't seem to care. They seemed content to have taken three. Felix was one of them. Just in the wrong place at the wrong time. I was there. I saw him, twisting and fighting to break away, but he was just a boy, and there were four of them dragging him."

Tommy was shocked and angry. He felt his hate for the Mother, which had been drifting in and out of his mind like the threat of a thunderstorm, begin to crystallize. "Shit la merde!" he said aloud without realizing it. "Frenna's son! He was learning English! *Shit la merde!* They stole her child! They probably raped his mind and plugged what was left into the Mother! The bastards!"

Harrison stopped shovelling. "Nope. They never got him." He was leaning on his shovel, breathing heavily, smiling crookedly. "Frenna. One shot. Fifty metres. Right in the head."

"Mr. Antikagamac, would you like to go for a little walk?"
Tommy had been so absorbed in the paper-book he had
been reading that he hadn't been aware of Lennox approaching.
He was sitting cross-legged on some mossy ground not far from
his tent. Flecks of sunlight danced on the ground as a light breeze
swayed the higher branches of the trees.

A rather odd invitation, he thought, wondering what Lennox
had in mind. "Sure," he answered. "Why not?" He tossed the book
onto a table in his tent, and then followed the older man along a
trail that led westward away from the camp.

"So, where are we going?"

"Tell me, Tommy, how are your headaches?"

"Gone. They've been gone for over a week."

"Good. Good. And are you still committed to staying with us,
as a Freeman?"

"I'm not going back to the Hive. That I am sure of. For now,
I'm content to stay here, in this 'outpost' of yours. Although I'd like

you to bring me to one of those 'enclaves' one of these days. I'd like to meet other Freemen."

"Of course, of course. In time. So you are committed to staying with us, even though you know we are hiding something from you."

Tommy's pulse jumped, although with an effort he showed nothing of his heightened attention. This whole concept of playing with hidden thoughts was new to him; he thought of it as a kind of game, which he found both perplexing and exhilarating. "Yes," he said after a few moments. "What choice do I have? I stay with you, or go back and get re-attached?" He spat on the ground. "No, I'm not doing that. I've known for some time that there is something going on here, that you aren't just scouting and mapping, and I suppose I'll find out in time."

"You spit on the Hive." Lennox chuckled.

"Damn right. I'm free now. My mind is my own. My thoughts are my own. My head is quiet, and it's mine, mine alone. In the Hive, your head does nothing but buzz and buzz and buzz with pointless babble. I'm free of that. And, yes, I spit on the Hive." He smiled and spat again.

"I, too, I spit on the Hive." Lennox himself expectorated, rather weakly, leaving a trail of spittle on his chin, which he wiped onto his sleeve.

"You call that a spit? If you're going to spit on the Hive, do it like you mean it!" Tommy inhaled deeply, and then spewed a great gob of saliva that arced 2 metres through the air. "That's how you spit on the Hive."

Lennox tried again, this time with a bit more power.

"Now *that's* a spit," Tommy exclaimed.

"Mr. Antikagamac, how would you like to do more than spit on the Hive?"

Tommy froze. He had been about to say something about Europeans being lousy spitters, but the thought fled from his mind. *How would you like to do more than spit on the Hive?* Shit *la merde!* He'd forgotten that these people were called Ketchen!

*

Tommy followed Lennox into the tent. Seated around a long table were eight people; standing at the head was a tall, thin man, bald on the top of his pate with wisps of grey-black hair around enormous ears, wearing spectacles that sat a bit crookedly on a large, hooked nose. Tommy recognized him as Hans Merck, his favourite cook.

Everyone in the tent had their eyes fixed upon the newcomer as if he'd just interrupted a private party. There wasn't a sound for a dozen long seconds.

"Please," Hans said at last, "sit."

Tommy self-consciously sat down next to Myles. Lennox had discreetly assumed a place at the end of the table opposite Hans.

Without preamble, Hans pushed a button on a device on the table, and a picture of some sort was projected in primitive fashion onto a screen. It took Tommy a few seconds to realize that it was a photograph of a small valley, mountains rising all around. Dominating the centre of the photograph was a large number of what looked like black pins of various sizes, some tens of metres tall, rising vertically from the valley floor.

"Ze *Getturmerk Array*," Hans said. "It measures 316 metres by 185 metres. It contains 1392 rorg-antennae varying in height from 2.8 metres to 48 metres. Zey support 464 nodes vis sree-fold redundancy."

"By nodes, he means a particular electromagnetic frequency," Lennox interjected for Tommy's benefit from the back.

"Uh, yes," Hans agreed, a bit piqued at the interruption.

"Each node can piggy-back up to 50 million signals, each one producing a unique beat signature . . ." Lennox continued, then stopped as he saw Hans glaring at him. "I'm sorry, Hans. Please go on."

Hans took a breath, "And of course," he said deliberately, his eyes fixed on Lennox, "zese signals are modulated to transmit information once zey are relayed srough a local hub. Ze modulation is done by introducing . . ."

"Come on," Ameline interrupted impatiently. "He doesn't need to know all this!"

Hans barked something back in German, to which Ameline responded likewise. Instantly, there were a half-dozen voices arguing over each other. A minute went by, the arguing becoming more and more intense and chaotic, until Tommy's level of discomfort reached a point that he could no longer tolerate. He rose from his seat and began to make his way out of the tent.

He was stopped, as was the hullabaloo behind him, by a sharp rapping on the table. Harrison, standing, had removed one of his shoes and had used it to bang the table-top.

"Shit's sake!" he shouted to the sudden lull. "Tommy, get back here. Everybody just shut up." He gestured sharply with his head to Tommy, who reluctantly returned to his seat. "Bunch of morons," he muttered. He looked at Tommy and pointed at the forgotten screen. "The *Getturmerk Array*," he said impatiently, in a manner that didn't invite questions. "It's like a medulla. It controls the microwave signals of the Mother for all of Western Europe."

"There are seven such arrays around the world . . ."

"Lennox, shut the fuck up!" Harrison glared at Lennox for a moment, then shook his head and sat down. He flicked his hand in the direction of Hans. "Hans, don't be an ass. Just tell him what he needs to know."

Hans waited petulantly for a few seconds before he stood up. He straightened his glasses. He pushed a button, and another photo came on the screen. It looked like a close-up of one of the pins, but then Tommy noticed that this one was a bit different from the others. It was thicker, for one thing. Near the top, there was a series of horizontal bars approximately a metre in length. Thick wires emerged from the base and disappeared into large metal containers that had been built into the ground nearby.

"Zis is ze timing tower," he said. Turning to Harrison, he added, "I hope zat's not too much detail." He looked back at Tommy. "Ze carrier signals must have a precise time signature. Zat is provided to ze local hubs from zis location, via satellite. Zere are 216 such satellites, each orbiting at twenty sousand kilometres vis an orbital speed of about four kilometres per second. Because of ze speed and ze veaker gravitational field at ze location of ze satellite, zere must be a relativistic time correction of 0.451 nanoseconds per second of time, according to ze eqvations of our good friend Herr Einstein. Furzer crosstalk among ze satellites narrows ze time error to ze order of picoseconds; zat's ze order of precision req-vired to make ze whole sing verk. But of course, you don't need to know zat. Ze point is, it is from zis location zat ve can cataclysmi-cally disrupt ze brain of ze Hive."

Tommy felt blood rushing out of his head; he almost lost his balance and fell from his chair. Had he heard correctly? *Cataclysmically disrupt the brain of the Hive.* Not: "Sabotage the Besançon Power Station" or "Damage the Eastern France Transportation System." *Cataclysmically disrupt the brain of the Hive.* To hear it articulated so nonchalantly . . .

What was he doing here? He was a football player, not a sabo-teur. He'd told Lennox he'd listen, listen to what they were plan-ning, but fully expecting to respectfully decline any invitation to be involved. Wasn't this a petty band of Ketchen, preparing some petty attack against their enemy, striking a blow that was about as effective as spitting on the ground? *Cataclysmically disrupt the brain of the Hive?* Who the hell *were* these people?

"... a magnetic field pulsed 0.002% below ze frequency of oscil-lation ..." Hans was still talking, but Tommy had missed what he was saying, perhaps even the last minute of explanation. It didn't seem to matter.

"Shit's sake, Hans!" he heard Harrison and others protesting. "He doesn't know a quantum number from his dick, and you're telling him about lepton spin-flips?" In another second, the meeting would once again deteriorate into chaotic squabbling.

"It's okay!" Tommy exclaimed, holding his hand up. The tent quieted. "It's okay. I'd like to know." He said this not just to defuse the impending argument, but because he was frustrated at being talked *about*, as if he were a person who was not there, as if he were a person who hadn't the brains to understand the subject matter. "Go ahead, go ahead Hans."

Hans smiled, and proceeded for the first time to talk to Tommy as if he were a student instead of a chair. "Ze atomic clock vich gives ze time signature is based upon a qvantum characteristic of a particular atom. Zis characteristic is robust and irrefutably repro-ducible. It is possible, however, to introduce a tiny alteration in zat characteristic, to ze part of about one vibration in a billion, srough ze use of a varying magnetic field tuned to ze proper frequency.

"Zat is vat ve intend to do.

"Ve have designed and built a small contraption zat vill produce ze necessary field. It simply needs to be placed near ze atomic clock, vich is about a metre underground at zis location" – Hans pointed at one of the metal containers beneath the large pin on the screen – "oriented in ze correct direction, and turned on. Vissin about sirty seconds, timing discrepancies will be large enough to affect ze Mozzer's signals; after two minutes zere vill be nossing but static.

"Do you have any qvestions?"

Tommy looked around at the ten other people in the tent, all staring back at him intently. "Who *are* you people?"

"Just a few people who vant to right ze vorld," Karl Schreibert replied obliquely.

"But . . . how do you know all this . . . How do you know . . . atomic clocks and magnetic vibrations and microwave signals and . . ." – Tommy gestured vaguely – "How do you know all this stuff?"

"We are scientists." This from Ameline.

"Physicists, more precisely," Lennox said. He opened his hand to indicate the people seated at the table. "I have recruited them all." He smiled crookedly as he leaned back in his chair. "The best minds in Europe. Chosen from the thousands of Freemen minds that have been forced by circumstances to think, to create, to initiate, to excel in order to survive, in order to thrive, just like minds throughout the history of humankind have done. Fire. The wheel. The printing press. The telescope. The atomic bomb. Ice cream. The minds of Freemen can run rings around the muddled mush that are the collective minds of your scientists in the Hive. Not because of genetic superiority, but simply because our minds are exercised in ways that were lost to the Hive decades ago, so many ways . . ."

"Oh, Lennox, will you cut the crap?"

"Am I not correct, Harrison? But perhaps my thesis will be better debated from the perspective of future generations. The point is,

Tommy, that we have been planning this . . . mission . . . for over five years. The technical details of the Getturmerk Array are readily available to anyone in the Hive. And any Freeman with a computer and an ability to break code. Herr Weiskopf, for example." Lennox nodded towards the young computer expert.

Tommy stared at the screen in amazement. "Wouldn't it be a whole lot simpler just to blow up the thing?"

"Before you could say your own name, the European lobe would switch to another array, probably Wisecastle in Newfoundland. It's automatic. The system can protect itself from any natural disaster imaginable, earthquake, volcano, swarm of metal-eating locusts . . . The arrays are mind-bogglingly robust, but on the infinitesimal chance that one fails, the other six can easily compensate. Responses would be slower – people would get annoyed because they might have to wait a couple of seconds to get their link to Annetta Diangelo or whoever the current darling of Hollywood is, but that's all that would happen. Three or four months of inconvenience until a new array is constructed.

"But with what we intend to do, there will be no such automatic protection measure because there will be nothing wrong with the array. Nothing. It will continue to function, but cease to be functional. It will be a disease in the Hive that will be most difficult to diagnose. The perfectly healthy Getturmerk Array will function as it always has, and in doing so, will block assistance from any other array. It will, ironically, prevent the Hive from being a hive."

Everyone was staring at Tommy. He felt as if he were an alien in the room. He had no doubt that what was being explained was correct, but nobody had addressed the question that to his mind was the most obvious.

"But why? Certainly they'll figure out what went wrong eventually, and fix the thing . . . I mean, so what? So you disrupt the system for a week or two . . . You cause havoc and mayhem, make a big mess of everything, get everyone angry and upset . . . It's simply destruction for the sake of destruction. It accomplishes nothing. I mean, I hate the Mother; I hate . . . well, not hate, but . . . I understand the shortcomings of what it is to be in the Hive. I see a reason for wanting to tear it apart and set people's minds free.

"In fact, I think I understand that even better than you people do . . . but what's the purpose of all" – he gestured at the screen – "this? It's not going to make people say, 'You know what? Let's disconnect all this Hive stuff and let's live as individuals, the way people did a century ago.' Are you kidding? It'll just get people angry. Real angry. And I can tell you what: as soon as they get everything back up and running, they'll come here and root you out for good. Don't underestimate the Hive. People will be so angry that they'll come and root you out. In the long run, you'll have done nothing except commit suicide. Certainly, if you have the brains to . . . do what you're planning to do, then you must have also figured out how pointless and stupid it is . . . So, why?"

"For one thing, Tommy, we estimate a month or two, rather than a week or two. Of course, maybe that's wishful thinking. But let's hope it's a month. Or two. Have you noticed what's happened to you in two months? Two months, Tommy, and you're as much a Freeman as any of us! Can you imagine if that happens to millions? Tens of millions? Hundreds of millions? Over half a billion people will be left connected to nothing, forced to think individually, forced to use their minds, forced to learn how to survive! After a month, how many will look around and see how much better off they are with their own thoughts and their own imaginings, how many will wonder how they could have allowed their minds and their lives to be shackled, how many will rise up to change things? This isn't a disruption we're planning, Tommy. It's a revolution."

Tommy put his hands over his face and rubbed his eyes. Too much to absorb. Too much. "Aren't you throwing a bunch of dice in the air and hoping they all come up sixes? I mean, what are the chances of *this*? And then *that*? And then *that*? If your plan works out to perfection, and in a month you have a hundred million people who want out of the Hive permanently, they're still a teacup beside a bucket. Eight billion people will swallow your revolution up like a bad meal. And then they'll come and destroy you. Us. Look, you're not going to beat the Hive; why not let them just lead their lives and let us lead ours?"

"Because ours are doomed." It was Harrison who had spoken.

Whenever Harrison opened his mouth, Tommy noticed, people listened. Lennox might have been the unofficial leader and organizer, and he might have been the philosophical vision-ary, but Harrison was the practical one, the one with common sense, the one people trusted despite his crustiness and his off-colour language. Tommy was beginning to understand the social dynamics of this little group of revolutionaries.

"We're disappearing. We can never grow; we can only lessen. And we lessen every year. In one generation, maybe two, perhaps in some remote region three, we will be gone. No more Freemen. There will only be the Hive, in all its tit-sucking numbness. Humankind's marvellous legacy: a cesspool of grey matter and pointless, trivial thoughts endlessly circulating and finding mean-ingfulness in themselves. Well, maybe we *are* hoping for a bunch of fucking sixes. You have a better idea?"

A good 20 seconds went by without a word or a movement. "What," Tommy finally said, "what does any of this have to do with me?"

Ameline stood up and walked to the head of the table. Hans moved and sat down on an empty chair on the side. Ameline clicked a button on the side of the projector, and yet another view of the array appeared on the screen. "Here is where we enter. *Ici.*" She used a red laser pointer to indicate a gate in the fence which surrounded the array. "A sensor-box here" – she pointed at something Tommy couldn't see – "controls the gate. It opens with a series of five microwave frequencies. We recorded those frequencies 20 months ago when they came to do an upgrade. They have come three times since then for maintenance or to install new pins; the same code opened the gate. So we are certain we can open it also.

"The problem is that an alarm will be set off exactly 12.0 seconds after the code to open the array is completed. It is not the sound of the alarm that is a problem; there is no one to hear it. But an alarm signal will instantly be sent to other parts of the Mother, and our mission is as good as dead. *Morte. Finit.*

"When they come to work on the array, a person with a transmitter sends out a signal once the gates are opened; the signal is received here." Ameline pointed her laser at a two-metre-tall metallic box near the centre of the array. "This is where the alarm is controlled. The transmitted signal turns it off. *Malheureusement*, we have been unable to determine the frequency of the signal that does this."

Another image came on the screen: a grainy close-up of the alarm box. "There is a manual switch on this side which shuts off the alarm. Last year, somebody screwed up with the transmitter, and the alarm went off by mistake. The workers were not very concerned, and one of them just walked to the box and pressed the button and shut it off. It was not a big deal; they made fun of the man with the transmitter and everyone laughed. But that is why we know that there is a 12.0-second delay, and that you can turn it off manually. We have also seen them turn the alarm off and on from this location to check it."

Ameline clicked the button, and an image of the array from still another angle was projected. She used her laser pointer to delineate a path on the screen with two right angles. "*Voici*. This is the most direct route from the gate to the alarm box. It is free of obstacles. Its length is 82.4 metres.

"That is what this has to do with you."

Tommy rubbed his eyes. Suddenly he felt intensely angry. "So this is what you've been keeping me for. This is why I was your prisoner. This is why you disconnected me. You haven't been 'correcting my mind' in order to free me; you've been brainwashing me so that I can be your tool."

"You haven't been brainwashed," Lennox said. "You know that. And we disconnected you long before we realized that freeing you from the Hive would have this . . . benefit. A week before, to be precise. It was Harrison who realized that you were an answer to a major problem we were facing. What we were doing to you, what we've done since . . . we would have treated you the same way if you'd been bred to play chess."

Tommy felt himself falling into the confused state from which he'd thought he'd finally emerged. Was everybody lying? Was he one of them? Was he their prisoner? Their pawn? Their compatriot?

"You said you ran the 100 metres in 8.8 seconds." Harrison ignored Tommy's obvious agitation. "I presume that was on a track with starting blocks. This is not a track. At least one second will go by before the gate is opened wide enough for you to get through. There are two turns, and a 3.7 metre change of elevation. I figure you'll have about one second to find and press the button that de-activates the alarm. We need you to run the path in at most 10.0 seconds."

"There's nobody else here that can even come close," Lennox added.

Tommy's head was pounding again. Just like *that*, the head-ache came back.

"You say I'm a free man. Well, what if I refuse? What if I say 'Screw it. I'm leaving.' Will you point your guns at me again? Threaten to shoot me if I don't comply? What will you do?" Tommy felt himself shouting. "Smash my head again? And what would you be doing if I hadn't stumbled into your hands? You might all be a bunch of geniuses; what were you planning to do? What? Were you all twiddling your thumbs waiting for somebody to stumble along who happened to run 100 metres in 8.8 seconds?" He knew he wasn't making any sense, but words kept spewing from his mouth without any conscious volition. He felt dizzy.

A hand was on his shoulder; it was Lennox. He realized that he had got to his feet, and now he looked around at the anxious faces staring at him. He saw fear; they were afraid of him. "I don't know," he mumbled forlornly. "I don't know anything."

"Sit down, Tommy."

"I don't know what I want." He allowed himself to be pushed back onto his chair.

"You said that you hated the Mother. That you wished every-one's minds could be free. That you would help the Freemen to survive. That you were glad to be one of us."

"I don't know what to think. What is right. Who to trust. I don't even know who I am!"

"You're Thomas Pierre Antikagamac, and you're a free man. I know this isn't easy. But you *are* free. You don't have to partici-pate. Whether you do or you don't, you're still welcome as one of us. You're still a Freeman. And if you want to leave, go back to the Mother, you can do that too. We hope you can help us out, but if you don't, *enh. Tant pis*. We can do this without you. We haven't been twiddling our thumbs. What were we planning to do? Some of us feel we should wait until we nail the frequency of the alarm transmitter; Roger believes he will get it the next time they come for maintenance in early November. More of us favour Harrison's idea; he's been working on a motorized bike. Both ideas are fraught with technical problems and uncertainties. Your fortuitous arrival gave us a new option, one we judged had a greater chance of success."

"I have to lie down. I have to think. I have to sleep."

"Go ahead, Tommy."

The big man got up slowly and left the tent, hunched as if he were carrying an enormous weight on his shoulders.

"Are we fucked?" Harrison said to Lennox when he'd left.

"No, I don't think so. No, my callous friend, I think we've got ourselves a runner."

*

When Tommy lay down on his bed, his mind was a maelstrom of thoughts and images. Despite feeling an overwhelming exhaustion, he tossed and turned for an hour before he fell asleep.

And when he woke up, with the pain in his head reduced to a little more than a dull ache, his mind was clear. Crystal clear. He stepped out of his tent. The sun hadn't risen yet, but there was enough morning light to make the sky above the trees a pale blue. The grass was damp with dew. He did 20 minutes of yoga, 100 sit-ups holding a rock to his chest, 20 one-legged squats with each leg, 15 one-handed push-ups with each hand, and then jogged along the trail out of camp until he came to a straight, horizontal section about half kilometre away. And there, with a rest of 30 seconds between each repetition, he sprinted 100 metres at 80 percent intensity 15 times.

With the help of Harrison, Myles, and a couple of Germans who didn't speak English, a path of sorts was fashioned in an area not far from the camp to match the parameters of the path in the array from the gate to the alarm box. The grade wasn't quite right, but they'd cut away branches and roots and removed some rocks, to the point where Tommy had a practice path that was a reasonable facsimile of that which he would have to run to get to the alarm. Eight metres, then a sharp right-hand turn. Fifty-seven metres, then a sharp left-hand turn. Eighteen more metres to the finish line.

The first time he ran it, he took 12.3 seconds.

"Shit," Harrison said.

"Well, this isn't exactly a track," Tommy answered.

After a five-minute rest, he ran it again, and then again, and then again. Each time the course was a bit more familiar, the footing a bit more secure, the direction changes more authoritative. On his fourth repetition, he clocked 11.5.

"That's it for today," he announced.

"That's it? Are you kidding?" Harrison was beside himself. "Four fucking runs? That's a pretty wimpy workout! You're supposed to be an athlete! Is this how hard you train for football? We spend three shitty days busting our asses making this track for you, and 'That's it for today'? Fuck me."

"Hey, hamstrings, man. I don't want to pop one of these suckers. I haven't sprinted in six months."

Harrison made a sound through his teeth and shook his head disgustedly, then headed back to the camp while Tommy sat on the ground to stretch.

To Harrison's chagrin, Tommy didn't race the course the next day, nor the day after that, nor even the day after that. Instead, he did drills, the same running drills he would use in his regular summer training before football camp began. He would jump vertically from one leg while bringing the other knee as high as possible, alternating legs; he would run as rapidly as possible but with short, 15-centimetre steps, knees coming to waist level, then the same drill but with his knees remaining downward, this time bringing his heels up to meet his buttocks; he would do lunges where he would drive forward horizontally with one leg, land, and then drive forward with the alternate leg; he would start running slowly and then gradually increase his speed until he was running smoothly and relaxed at 80 percent of his maximum; he would sprint hard from a standing start, but only for five strides. Harrison expected that after this warm-up, Tommy would then practice sprinting the whole course many times, but instead, Tommy would do a series of stretches and call it a day.

"You know nothing about training and peaking," he said in response to Harrison's complaints.

"I know a frigging lazy-ass when I see one."

On the fifth day, he did indeed run the course, but only at 80 percent of his maximum intensity. He did this 20 times, with a minute of rest between each run. "Fourteen point four seconds," Harrison would call after each one. "Come on, Anti-fucking-kagamac! Put some effort into it!" When he was finished, Tommy announced that he was taking the following day off. Harrison threw the watch he was holding onto the ground. "This is bullshit," he said.

Over the next couple of weeks, Tommy increased the intensity and the duration of his workouts. They became an hour and a half long, then two hours. Sometimes he doubled up morning and evening, adding an hour run along the trails. People would come to look, so that he often had six or seven people silently watching while he went through his stretches and his drills. Nobody said anything, not even Harrison. It seemed common sense not to interrupt a sweaty six-foot-eight football player at work. On the eighth day, he sprinted the course twice: 10.9 and 11.2 seconds.

On day 12, he ran 10.4, then on day 16, expecting to do better, he clocked 10.6. "Shit *la merde!*" he cried. He picked up a fist-sized rock and threw it angrily at a tree, hitting it dead centre, then stormed back to camp. No one dared say anything to him, not even Harrison. Myles and several of the observers went up to the tree, and Myles put his finger into the indentation the rock had made. It went in almost to the second knuckle

On day 21, the third of October, eight days before the planned attack on the array, he ran the course in 10.0 seconds.

*

It was still dim when they set out on the morning of October 10. There were 12 of them in the party: a stocky German in the lead, followed by Myles, Hans, Harrison, and Jacques Benoit, who

Tommy knew better as "The Kitchen Man" because he was often behind the serving table in the mess tent. The two women came next, Ameline and Frenna, then Karl, and finally Tommy, Lennox, Roger Lafontaine the pig farmer, and Neder Axel, who had frequently been one of Tommy's guards. They all carried packs or equipment, except for Frenna. Four of them had rifles strapped to their packs. They walked quietly, with the exception of Lennox, who talked incessantly.

The pace was not strenuous. In fact, Tommy found it to be rather plodding, to the point where he had to tell himself to be patient. Every two hours, they stopped to rest and drink. The autumn morning was cool, overcast at first but eventually turning to intermittent sun and cloud. The trail passed through forests and fields; when in the latter, Tommy felt tiny in the midst of the magnificent hills, which rose on one side, generally his left, and the valleys, which swept away on his right. The terrain where they walked was not particularly steep, not enough to give Tommy more than the occasional wave of his acrophobia. Lennox had assured him that the journey would not involve any precipitous terrain.

Shortly before noon, they entered a wooded area, and the trail began to wind uphill. Terrain became tricky, sometimes difficult, yet the pace remained as constant as a metronome. Tommy welcomed the increased exertion, even as he became aware of sweat forming on his brow. No one commented on the obvious change in intensity, so he didn't either. He knew he was with experienced hikers. His long legs were an advantage when large vertical steps were required, but the others in the company seemed to manage the path quite fine. For much of the time, his focus was upon the ground shortly ahead of him, watching the steps of Karl, but occasionally he'd look up and see Ameline and even Frenna negotiating an obstacle with surprising nimbleness.

They progressed in this fashion for about an hour, stopped for lunch, and then continued for another hour. When they emerged from the wood, the air was noticeably cooler, although the sun was shining brightly in a blue autumn sky. A stiff breeze made the grasses undulate. Grey peaks that had been a distant backdrop in the early morning were now looming weightily.

And within five minutes of leaving the wood behind, the green slope that the path traversed took on a spectacular vertiginous aspect that some would call breathtaking.

Tommy uttered a weak sound and shuddered. He felt his breath become shallow, and he stopped for a moment as a wave of dizziness swept over him. A gap opened up between him and Karl, and Lennox stopped behind him. He swallowed, and forced himself to move forward.

He didn't go very far before he stopped again.

"Are you all right, Tommy?" Lennox asked.

Tommy shook his head "no" quickly. He was staring at the ground in front of him. "You said there were no big heights," he said with a strained voice. Despite 130 kg of body mass, he felt the strong wind threaten his balance.

"You're scared of this? Come, now, Tommy, this is nothing. Really. People ski down slopes like this. Anyway, if it bothers you, just don't look down. Keep your eyes in front. And there's no way you're going to fall. I mean, look how wide the trail is: you could ride a horse along here."

The image of being up on the back of a horse at his present precarious location made his knees become watery. A gust of wind pushed him; he sucked air noisily between his teeth.

"What's going on?" Roger said from behind Lennox.

"I need room!" Tommy shouted, eyes still on the ground in front of his feet.

"Give him a moment," Lennox said quietly.

Tommy took several deep breaths, forcing himself to be calm. "Just..." – he held his hand behind him as if to ward off something evil – "just give me room." He hunched over, like he was trying to fit into a low-ceilinged room, and took a couple of tentative steps. Slowly, he raised his eyes. A large gap had opened between him and the others. The trail was clearly gaining elevation. "Shit," he said under his breath. "Shitshitshitshitshitshitshit." He looked back to the ground.

He tried to reason logically. "Nobody else seems to be fazed in the least," he said to himself. "Nobody else is scared. Don't be a coward. Don't make yourself an embarrassment. I'm a professional athlete. Look at Frenna. She's not scared. Hell, if *she* can do this, certainly I can as well. Just let me go slowly. And give me room."

He continued forward. "Does it get worse?" he asked Lennox, without altering his bent-over, eyes-to-the-ground posture.

"What?"

Lennox hadn't heard him. "Does it get worse?" he asked more loudly.

This time there was no answer at all. "Lennox!" he shouted, "Does it get worse!"

"You're doing fine, Tommy. Just keep going."

Tommy stopped again. "Are we going there?" He pointed to the grey rock faces that loomed ahead and to the left. He looked rather comical as he pointed uphill because he was still bent over and looking at the ground at his feet.

"It's an easy trail, Tommy. No ropes, no crampons . . . It's not dangerous at all. Really. Trust me."

But Tommy had already decided that he could go no further. Lennox was right beside him, Roger, Neder, they were almost on top of him, the wind, the wind! He felt himself stumble . . . "Get back!" he shouted, sinking to his knees. He grabbed hold of tufts of grass on the uphill side of the trail. He was shivering.

Roger and Lennox were talking heatedly. Then Roger put two fingers to his lips and whistled loudly to the hikers up ahead.

"What's with him?" Karl asked when they had returned. Lennox answered in German, to which the whole group responded with a collective groan.

"You can't be serious," Harrison said. "Fuck sake, Tommy, we're not asking you to climb a cliff. It's a day hike along an easy trail. My grandmother could do it." Tommy said nothing, just shook his head. "Aahh!" Harrison waved his hand dismissively.

Ameline stepped next to Tommy. "This is not coward. This is stupid. Look at you. You look like a baby."

He didn't need to be told. He felt profoundly foolish, embarrassed, silly. He wished he could get up. He wished they would give him space. He wished the wind would stop. He wished . . . He realized that he wished he was connected to the Hive.

"I'll take him back." He heard Frenna's voice. "We can go around by the Weigen Trail. It gets us there just the same."

"It doesn't get you there the same," Hans countered. "It will take you three days."

"Two days. You go ahead, take your time, get everything ready. Me and Tommy will get there two days after you do, that's all."

"Two days, a hundred days, we still miss T-Day."

"Is that really so important?"

There followed a rather heated argument in German, which went on for several minutes. Finally, Harrison looked down to Tommy, who was still kneeling and sitting on his heels. "Let's go," he said. The group had already begun walking back along the trail in the direction from which they'd come.

*

They arrived at the array early afternoon of October 14, two days after T-Day. Tommy, Harrison, Myles, and Neder had actually gone right back to the base camp to pick up more supplies, and had hiked at a rather vigorous pace to catch up to the others. The site where they had all camped the night of October 13 was an unlikely one, hardly a "site" at all – a rocky, uneven area hidden within dense forest. The idea was that after the sabotage was completed, they would high-tail it back to the site and lie still for a couple of days, just in case, for some reason, the sabotage became known.

The sabotage itself wouldn't take long, although Tommy only had a vague idea of how it would actually be done. His job was to turn off the alarm; once that task was completed, he was no longer part of the equation. The "device" was essentially a half-cylinder, perhaps 20 centimetres in diameter and a metre in length, with six "feet" that emerged like the legs of a lizard. Harrison and Hans would be responsible for setting the device; its precise location and orientation relative to the – whatever it was that was buried just underground – would be established by signals read upon four hand-held receivers held nearby by Benoit, Karl, Neder, and the German whose name he had forgotten. The cylinder would be carefully placed as closely as possible to its correct position, and then micro-dials on each of the legs would be adjusted manually to give the cylinder its final precise direction, elevation, roll angle, and tilt. Myles and Ameline would be analyzing some sort of feedback information and calculating amplitude strengths and frequencies. Whatever all that meant. If it made sense to them, it was fine with him.

It was grey, and it was windy. There was a smell of approaching rain in the air. The wind was cool, but there was a faint sheen of sweat on Tommy's face. He had been running, back and forth beside the fence that enclosed the vertical needles of the array. Hundreds of them, incongruous against the wild mountain background with their precision and their hint of technological mastery. They were a lot taller than he had expected them to be, taller and shinier and, he had to admit, more intimidating. Here was a lobe of the brain of the Mother, and he felt as insignificant and as unwelcome as an ant in her bed.

And they were going to try to destroy her? For a moment, the immensity of the crime they were about to commit overwhelmed him. He was breathing too quickly, too shallowly; he forced himself to reduce his respiration rate. He had been running to warm up, he had stretched, and now he was doing some dynamic exercises to prepare his muscles for the explosive movements to come. Just like he would do before taking the field to quarterback the London Knights.

He was by himself; the others were standing about 50 metres away, watching him impatiently. Well, they would just have to wait. If he didn't do this right, they could all kiss this mission goodbye. It depended upon him.

Finally, when he felt that his muscles were ready, he sat on the ground, lotus position, back straight, head up, shoulders back. He closed his eyes. Before a game, he would sit like this for five minutes, music in his ears, while he reviewed the game plan details, the opposing defensive alignments, the blitzes, the pass defences he would face: all these would be provided to his mind's eye with a clarity that was more vivid than reality. Now, he saw nothing. With no connection, nothing came to his mind's eye, except what he conjured up himself. He visualized the path he would follow, 8 metres, a sharp right-hand turn, 57 metres, a sharp left-hand turn, 18 more metres. It was so vague, so dull. The box where the switch was. He tried to see it, really see it, but it was like trying to draw a picture of a smell. It just wasn't there. He opened his eyes. It was time.

He nodded, and the others came up alongside him.

"All right," Harrison said. "Ten seconds once you're inside. Don't trip, don't slip."

Tommy nodded.

"You can do it, son," Lennox said. Tommy nodded again. In the back of his mind, he registered the fact that Lennox had never called him "son" before.

He saw Frenna. She put her hands together, fingers interlaced, and shook them. She smiled. Tommy nodded to her as well. Then he turned to Harrison. "Let's go," he said.

He took a position next to the gate, ready to squeeze inside the instant it opened enough for him to get his body in.

One second to get in, ten seconds to get to the box, one second to hit the switch.

"Ready?" Miles said. "Here goes. It'll open on the fifth." On his transmitter, he dialled up a particular microwave frequency, then pressed a button. "One," he said. He repeated with a second frequency, then a third, then a fourth. Then he dialled up the fifth frequency, and pressed the button.

That's when all hell broke loose.

*　　*　　*　　*　　*

PART 2

1

Tommy heard the humming even as Myles was saying "Three," but didn't realize it. Perhaps it is more accurate to say that he felt it, rather than heard it, through his feet and in his chest. Later, when he thought back to this moment, he realized that he had in fact been hearing something, a vibration deep and menacing as if the Earth itself were grumbling, for several seconds before Myles dialled the fifth frequency, but he had been so intent on his task, so focused upon his sprint, that the sound didn't pierce his consciousness. Perhaps if it had, perhaps if they had had five more seconds of warning, five seconds more to run, things would have been different. But nobody else had his hearing; nobody else heard anything until it was too late.

When Myles pressed the button for the fifth frequency, the gate did not open. Nothing happened. But the sound, the vibration, had now become loud enough for them all to hear. They looked at each other anxiously. Tommy heard Ameline meekly say, "*Quoi?*" The air itself seemed to be throbbing. Tommy remembered it as if time had stretched for quite some length, but in fact it was only a couple of seconds. Harrison scrutinized the sky. "SHIT!" he yelled, and at that instant five enormous black buzzard helis of the type Tommy had only seen in books rose above the hills that surrounded the valley. The buzzards converged on their location with surprising speed, even while Myles was asking, "How? How? How did they know?"

Harrison whipped around and glared at Tommy with furious eyes. "You fucking traitor!"

"It wasn't me!" Tommy protested, even now not quite sure what was happening.

"Run! Idiots! Run!" Ameline was shouting. In fact, everyone seemed to be shouting something, but the sounds were all but drowned by the enormous thrumming of the big birds. The buzzards were closing in, surrounding them, and people were running pell-mell in an attempt to get to the woods, which were about 200 metres from the fence. Now troopers were in the air, disgorged from the bellies of the aircraft, steering to the ground with their jet packs, 20 of them from each craft. The German whose name Tommy never knew was on his knees with his rifle, firing away. And then before Tommy's eyes, he exploded, just like that. He was a human being, and then he was disintegrated flesh propelled in all directions.

Tommy put his head down and sprinted like he had never done before. He heard other gunfire, more explosions. There were troopers ahead and to his left, trying to cut him off, but he was zig-zagging like he would have done on the gridiron, the goal line of the forest just 20 metres away.

He heard a scream. Frenna! He cut sharply to his right, and there she was face down on the ground, back about 50 metres from the woods. She tried to get up, but there was something very wrong with her leg, she must have tripped in a hole, perhaps broken a bone, and now the troopers were on her, two of them, each holding an arm. She was writhing to escape like a fish on a hook. "NO!" Tommy shrieked as he ran in her direction. "NO! NO!" And then what felt like a hot spear pierced him between his shoulder blades, his arms and legs convulsed in electric shock, and his world became black before his face hit the ground.

*

Bright. So bright. His eyes were closed, but still the light hurt them. He wanted to keep his eyes shut, but they seemed bent upon opening of their own volition. He clamped his hands over them, rubbed them, then opened them to slits behind his hands. He saw orange along the lines where his hands' seal against the light was imperfect. He moved one hand so he could see through a crack between the hand and his nose. He made the crack a bit wider. He saw the corner of a desk, a great wooden desk with the rich colour of rosewood. Farther away was a wall, with some sort of artwork in a frame part way up. He moved his hand more. There was a lamp on the desk, an old-fashioned type with a copper-coloured stem and a green shade. There was a man sitting in a chair. Tommy himself was sitting, he realized, and the man was looking at him. Smiling. The man was perhaps in his early fifties, thinning brown hair cut short and brushed neatly, blue eyes behind black-framed glasses, a sharp-looking red unitop with black trim on the shoulders. Tommy slowly removed his hands completely from his eyes. The room wasn't as bright as he had first thought; the lighting was, in fact, rather muted. In different circumstances, it might have been pleasant. The picture on the wall was a painting of a landscape, a rolling green field with trees on one side, a curving dirt roadway, and three horses grazing freely in the background. There was another painting on the wall as well, this one of a pack of horses running right to left across a field of snow. There was a cabinet of sorts, constructed of wood the same colour as the desk, with a variety of vaguely scientific-looking items displayed on the shelves.

The man just continued to smile at Tommy, like some sort of benevolent ruler. It was quiet. No, not quite; there was soft music in the background, some of that archaic music that was played with violins and such.

It dawned on him that he was still alone in his head. They hadn't reconnected him. He was still free, at least to a certain extent.

"Where am I?" Tommy asked at last.

"You're home, Mr. Antikagamac."

"That doesn't help me much."

"Okay. London. Elizabeth II Square. The same place you were introduced to your new fans after you were traded here, what: three and a half years ago? Stoddard Building. Nineteenth floor, Room East 1927."

Tommy looked around uncertainly. There was a small round table to his left with two leather chairs with armrests, identical to the type that he and the man in front of him were sitting upon. Against the wall to his right was a bookshelf with paper-books. Real paper-books, pristine and expensively bound, like what might be found in a museum.

The two of them were alone.

"Who are you? What am I doing here?" Then, with sudden agitation, "Where are the others?"

The man put up his hand. "Forgive me. I'm not thinking straight. I have to admit I'm more than a little overwhelmed to be sitting opposite someone of your celebrity. Not that I'm a fan of American football, I'm not. To tell you the truth, I hate the game. Nevertheless, you're Tommy Pierre Antikagamac.

"My name is Shripton. Edgar Cornelius Shripton. And you're here because I asked for you. They're going to take you in a few minutes, I'm afraid, and you are going to be subjected to some rather unpleasant things. I can't help that." He reached into a drawer and took out two tumblers and placed them in front of him. Then he pulled out an expensive-looking bottle half-filled with amber liquid. "Scotch?"

Tommy shook his head impatiently. Shripton poured a quarter of a tumbler for himself. "Today's my mother's birthday. Eighty-three years old, the doll. She still sings with her choral society . . ."

"Are you going to reconnect me? You bastards?"

"Mr. Antikagamac," the man said, leaning forward, "you don't know me from Lassie, but you can trust me on this: I will not let you become reconnected, unless you yourself decide that is what you want. It will be your decision, no one else's. I guarantee it. And I do carry some authority around here."

"Where are the others?"

"I won't lie to you. Four of your party were killed. Ones who were shooting to kill your rescuers. But the rest were taken without injury."

"Rescuers. Right. Where are they? Have you recon-nected them?"

"They're fine."

"Fine. Fine where?"

"They're fine, Mr. Antikagamac," – then, in a louder, annoyed voice, he addressed somebody in the room behind Tommy – "You're early!"

"I'm sorry, sir. Do you want us to wait outside?"

Shripton shook his head. "No," he said, still clearly annoyed. "No, go ahead."

Tommy felt a hand on his shoulder. Men wearing blue unitops were on either side of him. "Mr. Antikagamac, sir, come with us, please." Two other men stood in the doorway. They had electric pistols attached to their waists.

*

The pain was like what you feel when you bang your funny bone; that is, the ulnar nerve on the inside of your elbow, tucked inside a bony protuberance called the medial epicondyle. If you are unfortunate enough to hit that nerve (and it's happened to everyone at some time or other) you feel a raw, electric pain that radiates down your arm to your little finger. Very unpleasant; hence, the absurd moniker "funny bone." Yes, the pain was like that.

Only worse.

And it wasn't his elbow. It was the place in his chest where he'd once broken a rib.

Tommy hadn't expected it, and he let out a yelp before he had time to steel himself.

"That was level 15, Mr. Antikagamac."

The man who spoke was standing about 3 metres in front of Tommy. He wore a blue unitop, as did the other two men in the white-walled room. One was seated at a console, and the third, who had three short horizontal black bars on the left breast of his shirt, stood with folded arms by a door.

A bright light was directed into Tommy's eyes, and they were watering. He squinted them closed.

"This next will be level 20." He could have been pointing out objects in a shop window.

Tommy braced himself, but still couldn't contain a groan when the pain hit him in the chest again. Sweat broke out on his forehead. He was standing, shackles on each wrist and each ankle.

The shackles were attached to flexible tubes of some sort, with only enough leeway to allow about 30 centimetres or so of movement in any direction, and strong enough to restrain any movement beyond that. The ones on his wrists had his arms forming a Y with his body.

"The highest level is 100, but we won't be using that. Level 100 will kill you."

Tommy certainly hadn't expected this turn of events. He had expected to have simply been reconnected to the Hive; end of story. Now he was afraid. Very afraid. But he was also defiant. And angry. Angry as hell.

"Why are you doing this?" he shouted. "Some pointless idea of punishment? You crank up the numbers and torture me until I scream, 'Sorry! I'm sorry!'? To what purpose? I'll say it now, if you want. What the hell difference does it make? It doesn't change a flea's testicle. You've caught us; we're done. After we're reconnected, the whole world gets a thrill to know how much pain we suffered for our crimes? Isn't your society supposed to be beyond that?"

An electric pain hit him in his left hip, radiating down the outside of his thigh to his knee.

"Level 15," the man in front of him said.

Another sharp pain, this one centred in his left ankle.

"Level 20."

Shoulder. Elbow. Groin. Neck. Twenty times he was subjected to electric nerve pain. The whole thing took about five minutes. Then a button was pressed, the shackles fell away and receded into slots in the floor and ceiling, and the man said cheerily, "That's it for now, Mr. Antikagamac." Just like a doctor after his pre-season medical.

Fifteen minutes later, he was back where he had regained consciousness what: an hour earlier? Except now he was alone in the room. The two tumblers and the bottle of Scotch were still on the desktop, one with just a trace of liquid in it. After the room in which he had been tortured, the light here was distinctly subdued. Classical music still played softly. There was a fish tank along one of the walls that Tommy hadn't noticed earlier. He was looking at aimlessly meandering tropical fish when Shripton entered through a side door.

"Back already?" he said pleasantly. "I hadn't expected you quite so quickly. Please, please. Have a seat." Shripton sat behind his desk. Tommy remained standing. "You're probably ready for that Scotch now."

Tommy turned away from the fish tank sharply. "Why aren't *you* connected? Whatever this" – he waved his hands vaguely – "this place is. Why is nobody seeing this? Why are you torturing me? What's going on here?"

Shripton had his hand up. "In time. In time. In time."

"You know, you were my son's favourite ceeb. He actually cried when they gave up looking for you." Shripton poured some brandy into the second tumbler and pushed it across the desk towards Tommy. Tommy ignored the offer.

Shripton gestured vaguely towards the ceiling, from which the light music, piano now, was emanating.

"Do you like Bach? I love Bach. These are the Goldberg Variations, an aria followed by 30 variations. And this is a masterful rendition by an artist from your own country of origin: Glen Gould. Have you heard of him? This is from a recording made over a century ago so, of course, the sound quality is rather lacking; nevertheless, you can't miss the fact that you are listening to genius, both composer and artist, can you?" Shripton closed his eyes for a moment and smiled as he listened to the music.

"I'm sorry," he said, looking again at Tommy. "I know you have all kinds of questions.

"Let's see: Your team, the London Knights, has won three and lost two. Bobby Sanders, your backup, is the team's quarterback. People are saying that without you the team may not get out of the West Europe Conference. Janet Eisenhower has a new number one hit. She's now living with Bobby Muggles, her manager, although she is still married to Constance Merriweather. Constance, meanwhile, is very happy mothering Ashley Pink's young boy, despite the fact that her former lover seems to have little interest in her anymore.

"Uzaki Ming scaled Everest in 4 hours 27 minutes, giving East Asia Typhoon the Cross-Games championship. Maria Piñata won the swimsuit award in the . . ."

"Will you cut the crap!" Tommy suddenly burst out, jumping up from his seat. With his towering height, he loomed over Shripton, who paused for a moment and then took off his glasses and wiped them with a white handkerchief that he had taken from a drawer.

"Mr. Antikagamac, please sit down."

"No! I'm not going to sit down!"

"Very well." Shripton put his glasses back on. "I'm sorry. I have an unfortunate tendency towards cynicism. My wife keeps reminding me. These were all among your favourite ceebs. Now . . . they pale beside Bach, don't they?" He leaned back in his chair. "You are going to be here for some time, Tommy. Here, that is, in our institute. We are here to help you. At this moment, you may not believe that, and that is understandable. You believe that we are here to punish you, and that is wrong. You were a victim of circumstances; you did nothing worthy of punishment. You think we will reconnect you to the Hive." He shook his head. "You will make that decision yourself. If you wish to reconnect, now or sometime in the future, it will be done. But it will be your choice. We won't force you."

"What bullshit. '*We won't force you*,'" Tommy mocked. "You'll just keep me prisoner and torture me until I give in, is that the game? Let's just cut the crap and get it over with."

"You are at most only partly correct, and a small part: you are, true, a prisoner, for a time. That's hardly what you would call unfair treatment; after all, you were caught in the act of rather substantial sabotage. But the term 'torture,' if not totally incorrect, is at best imprecise. Oh, I'm not a big proponent of the physical unpleasantness to which you will be subjected in the coming days, but it does have a purpose. Think of it as training. Training camp. As for your 'giving in,' that's not right at all. I, personally, will be very disappointed if you 'give in,' Tommy. I want you to stand firm. I want you to be strong. We will let you join the Hive only when you demonstrate that you really want to do so. It will be your decision."

He nodded to someone behind Tommy.

"Mr. Antikagamac?" came the same voice that had spoken to him earlier. "I'll show you to your quarters."

2

His "quarters" consisted of a 5 metre by 3 metre room furnished with a thin mattress on a wooden bed, a blanket folded at the end with a pillow on top, and a small table and chair. There was a vase with yellow flowers on the table. The walls and ceiling were white. There were no windows.

He was tired. Intensely tired. The after-effects of whatever it was that had knocked him out, he figured. He flopped onto the bed. His feet extended over the end, but at the moment, he didn't care. He needed sleep like he needed oxygen.

The sound coming from *this* ceiling certainly wasn't Bach. It was faint; in fact, he hadn't even noticed it when he first came in. But now, as he lay on the bed, he found it irritating. At first, it was merely mildly annoying, but soon it became intensely so. It wasn't even music. It wasn't simple noise, either. Disjointed sounds without context, overlapping, some vaguely similar to musical instruments, some machine-like, some electronic, and some that were beyond any sort of description at all assaulted his ears like tiny pins and needles. Irregular beeping noises played dissonantly over what might have been violins alternating high and low notes, while a heavy hum like the drone of one of those awful Scottish bagpipes became an organ sound, which then became a sound something like a helicopter. Suddenly, everything ceased, and the quiet was like a caress to his ears. For only a second, however, because then he was assailed by a series of single notes, which might have come from a piano, the notes coming with shorter and shorter intervals, while in the background was a throbbing sound like the engine room of a large 20th-century ship. There were ticks – tic-tic-tic-pause-tic-tic-tictictictic-pause-ticaticaticaticati-catica . . . There was the sound of a gong, which persisted for five minutes. Was that the sound of the bleating of a sheep? No. No, it would have been so much less unpleasant if he could identify the sounds, if he could relate them to something familiar, but he couldn't. There was no rhythm, no structure of which to grab hold, no consistency. It was worse than random: it was anti-music.

He got up and passed his hands all over the white walls, on the extremely unlikely possibility that there might be some sort of hidden control somewhere. There was no identifiable source of the music; it seemed to come from everywhere in the ceiling at once. As he stood looking up, he was struck by how quiet the sounds really were – it was practically nothing at all. Certainly he could ignore something so mild.

But as he lay on his bed and tried to sleep, his feet over the end, the music found him. It wriggled into his auditory canals like earwigs. How could he relax with bugs gnawing his eardrums? He turned onto his stomach and put the pillow over his head. Still, the music found him.

He may have dozed; he wasn't sure. Three men with blue unitops were in the room, asking him politely if he could "Please, come with us."

Down the hall to the elevator, a very brief *whoosh,* moving upward, and then along to a room with E544 beside the door-frame. The torture room.

The session was similar to his first: the shackles, the bright light, three men (not the same as those who had brought him there), polite and unemotional as they administered level 15s and level 20s. Then he was returned to his room, E311.

The music was still there.

"Can I have this blasted noise turned off?"

"Sorry, Mr. Antikagamac."

They came back again, what, two hours later? Three hours? The same routine. This time, Tommy protested vigorously and rather profanely.

"I'm sorry, Mr. Antikagamac."

And so it went on. In his room, Tommy would stuff a pillow over his head and try to sleep; before he could achieve a sound rest, he was awoken and brought to room E544.

The fifth time it happened, he refused. "No!" he said. He towered threateningly over the three men who had come for him; his fists looked like they could smash their heads in one wallop. "This circus ends now. I'm not going. Tell your Mr. Shripton that I've had enough of this nonsense. I don't know what he's expecting from me, but the next time I go to that room, you're going to have to drag me. And believe me, it's going to take a whole lot more than three of you."

The pain on his former rib injury was so exquisite that he blacked out for a moment. He was on his knees, each arm over the back of a blue-uniformed man on either side of him as they tried to lift him to his feet. The third held his electric pistol calmly at his side.

"I'm sorry, Mr. Antikagamac."

There was no sense of time in his world, nothing other than his pulse upon which to judge intervals. The infuriating music never ceased. Meals appeared; he ate joylessly. His exhaustion increased. Whenever he slept, his rest was interrupted for a trip to room E544. The men he saw changed; he was the only constant. He tried to keep track of days, but he could hardly even guess. Was it four now? Five, six, a week? Two weeks?

Two weeks. It must be two weeks. Why? What was the purpose of all this? What did they want from him? What did they want him to do? Renounce his sins? Agree to reconnect to the Hive? At this point, he figured, why not? What else was there for him to do? But even that didn't seem to be an option; it seemed as if his purpose was to serve as a plaything for these people. Why were they doing this?

He was sure that two weeks had gone by when, this time, the *whoosh* of the elevator was an instant longer than usual, and he found himself on the nineteenth floor rather than the fifth. His escort brought him to Room E1927.

Shripton was behind his desk, waiting for him.

"Good day, Mr. Antikagamac. You look exhausted, but I suppose that's to be expected. Are they providing you with enough food?"

"Fuck off."

"I won't take that personally because I know that's not really you speaking. You'd never use that language if you were properly rested."

"I don't care what you think. I've had enough. I want out. You guys win. Reconnect me."

"Don't be so quick about it, Tommy. You're not ready yet."

"Quick? I've suffered through your torture for two weeks. You don't let me sleep. The noise is driving me insane . . ."

"Two weeks? Tommy, it's only been three days."

Tommy stopped speaking and stared back at Shripton. Three days? Three *days? This . . . has only been going on for three days?*

He remembered one time he had thought he'd run the last of a series of training camp wind sprints, then the coach told him he was only half-way through. That was nothing.

Well, this was one set of wind sprints he had no intention of completing. What was the point?

"What difference does it make? Three days, two weeks, a year . . . I want out of this prison. I've paid enough for my crime."

"I'm surprised. You're the first. I thought you'd hold out the longest. None of your friends have given in yet."

Tommy caught his breath. The others. The slosh that had been his mind the last . . . three days . . . hadn't allowed him to think about the rest of his group. But of course: they were here too! And they were being tortured just like he was.

"I want to see them."

"I can arrange that." Shripton pressed a button. A moment later, he talked into a console that was angled towards him at the side of his desk. "Fennerty, get Ms. Gurdwald, room E421. Just take her out into the corridor."

Two things shook Tommy simultaneously. Ms. Gurdwald – Frenna – was here, one floor above his. But what was even more startling was what Shripton had just done: he needed an interface to communicate! People here were not even connected with each other! He knew already that Shripton and all the other blueshirts couldn't be connected to the Hive, at least, not in a normal way; otherwise, people would be aware of what went on here. But they couldn't even communicate with each other without an intermediate mechanism. Tommy had never seen people communicate with an external electronic device before.

"Come." Shripton was already getting up from his desk.

Tommy followed him, and once in the corridor outside the office, two others, electric pistols at their sides, fell into step behind them both. The elevator was a short walk away, and seconds after Shripton said, "Four," they were exiting onto a floor with door numbers in the 400s. Shripton stopped after about 10 steps. A door 15 metres away slid open, and out stepped a blueshirt, followed by Frenna and another blueshirt.

Frenna! Tommy's breath caught in his throat. She looked haggard, exhausted, *old*. *Bastards are torturing her just like they are me*, he thought with disgust. He realized that he probably looked as bad to her as she did to him. He made an effort to straighten up and appear strong. She was limping; something was wrong with her leg. He remembered: she had injured it in the field, trying to escape. Just then her eye caught his, really caught it, and in that eye was a look of strength, a look of defiance. At the same time, she shook her head, a barely perceptible movement, hardly a movement at all, but a movement, a direct communication, that had all the power of a shout. She hadn't given in, and she was telling him not to give in either.

He started to say something, her name, but before any sound came out, the blueshirt beside him said, "Please don't speak, Mr. Antikagamac." Polite, cool, and laden with threat.

Shripton must have given a nod because in an instant Frenna was returned to her room and Tommy's group was turning back towards the elevator.

"So, as you can see, she is here and she is, for the most part, healthy. Unfortunately, she suffered a very serious leg injury, and we are treating her. The rest of your group is also here, uninjured. For now, they are receiving similar treatment to yours, although this will change in the future. There are two of them about whom I have some concern; your friends Harrison and Ameline have both required two pistol shots. But I'm hopeful they'll be okay."

They were back on the elevator, Shripton said, "Nineteen," and after a short *whoosh!* they were again on the nineteenth floor. "The treatment you are receiving, Tommy, is called PRADIT, which is an acronym for one of those silly grandiose phrases designed to impress people. Progressive something or other; I could never be bothered with remembering it. At any rate, I know PRADIT is unpleasant, but believe me, we wouldn't subject you to it unless it was the *least* unpleasant, not to mention the most effective, way to reintegrate you into the Hive. We . . ."

"I don't want to be reintegrated into the Hive!" Tommy cried loudly.

They were back at E1927; with a *fff023tt*, the door opened by sliding silently into the wall, and then *fff023tt*, it closed behind Tommy as he followed Shripton. The blueshirts stayed outside.

"I understand." Shripton picked two golf clubs, putters, from a rack beside the door that Tommy hadn't noticed before. "Golf?" he said, offering one to Tommy. The big man ignored the gesture, and Shripton returned one club to the rack.

"As I said, you don't have to rejoin if you don't want to. It's your choice. No one will coerce you. It will always be your choice alone." While he was speaking, he took a golf ball from a tray beside the rack and set it on the carpeted floor.

"Real choice," Tommy said sarcastically. "Torture me until I can't take it anymore and say 'Give!'"

"Not at all. You'll see." Shripton lined up a putt, aiming at a contraption on the floor about 5 metres away that served as a hole. He struck the ball, then grimaced as the ball stopped a good metre short of the target.

"PRADIT aside, I want to make sure that you are being well-cared-for. That's why I asked you if you were getting enough food. Someone your size – you probably eat twice as much as someone like me." He took another ball from the tray and offered his club to Tommy, who again ignored the gesture. Shripton set the ball on the floor. "Are you comfortable? Aside from the electronic music . . ."

"No, no, I love the music."

Shripton made another putt; this one missed to the right and stopped 50 centimetres beyond the target. "*Bullocks,*" he said quietly, then, "Sorry about that." He took a third ball. "Seriously, though, anything you can think of. Meanwhile, I'm going to invite you here from time to time to . . ."

"My bed," Tommy interrupted.

"Bed? You want something softer?"

"Longer."

"Oh, bloody hell. Did they give you a regular-sized bed?"

"I assumed it was part of your torture."

"Consider it replaced. Not that you get to enjoy it very much, but I'll get you a 250-centimetre bed." Shripton bent over his putter. "You probably have blank walls, too. I bet the idiots put you into a standard room." He took a putt; the ball stopped 15 centimetres to the left of his first one.

"Oh, balls," he said, putting the putter back onto the rack. "I hate this game. I can't understand why people like it. Did you know that golf is the third most followed sport in the world, after your American football and after baseball? Blows me away." He went to pick up the three golf balls. "My oldest son wants me to play with him. Birthday present. I'm going to be 52 next week . . ."

"A paper-book," Tommy interrupted.

"I'm sorry?"

Tommy gestured towards the bookcase. "I want a paper-book."

"Certainly. Although you won't have much time for one . . . To clarify: paper-book or real book?"

Tommy gestured to the bookcase again. "Paper-book."

"Very well. And good for you. I'm impressed. I really am. You will want to be continuing with *Treasure Island*, I suppose?"

Tommy's mouth dropped open. There was a pause of 10 seconds before he spoke.

"How . . . how did you know? I wasn't connected. You shouldn't know . . . I wasn't attached to the Mother . . ."

"Tommy, the connections between an individual's brain and the Mother are very . . . complex. Mr. Voight is a very good doctor, considering the Ketchen have no medical school. Nevertheless, he is far from capable of completely removing all connections to, well, us. You *were* detached from the Hive, but the Hive isn't quite everything."

"So it *is* through me that you caught us. You found us through *me! I* betrayed the group . . ."

"Hardly, Tommy. Don't feel any guilt. They would not have been able to do it without you anyway."

"But I don't understand! If there was still a contact with me, why didn't you rescue me? You could have rescued me and reconnected me long before any of this happened, long before I ever met any Ketchen . . . Why didn't you rescue me right away, as soon as the glitch happened? I don't understand!"

"Tommy, who do you think it was that caused your glitch in the first place?"

$\}$

Tommy committed himself to keeping better track of time, but he wasn't successful. In his windowless, constantly illuminated room, there was no concept of day or night. He had no idea of how long his sleeps were, as he was always awakened by the blueshirts before his rest was complete. The time intervals between trips to E544 seemed to be almost random: sometimes he might have been in his room for only 10 minutes, other times perhaps several hours. The shock levels were no longer level 15 and level 20; they had increased first to 20 and 25, and now they were levels 25 and 30. Each five-minute "treatment" finished with him soaked in sweat. When he slept, he would dream vague things, which would coalesce into a sharp jolt of pain, and he would find himself jerked awake by the dream despite his fatigue. And the endless un-rhythmic ticks and hums and discordant musical noises that he could barely hear but could not ignore . . . he just wished they would go away away away . . . Fatigue enveloped his mind like mud. How long would it go on? Forever? Or until he was mad with despair? Pain without end, fatigue with no hope . . .

Only the vision of Frenna's defiant eyes, the quick shake of her head compelling him to hold on, to *not give in*, kept him from folding in upon himself. *Hold on*, he would tell himself fiercely while an ever more powerful voice in his head called out, *What for? How long?* He did mathematics exercises: $13^2 + 18$. $(x + 3)$ $(x - 5)$. The volume of his room. He found it more and more difficult to concentrate, more and more difficult to hold things in his head. If he saw Shripton again, he would ask for paper and a writing implement.

He had been moved to a different room, one with a bed that provided several centimetres of extra length beyond his body. The walls were not blank: there were three screens, each a metre by two. Two of the screens showed three-dimensional static images of cute cats or magnificent waterfalls or extraordinary gardens, the images fading one into the next every three seconds. The third was a jennix, one of those sensational 3-D sensurworld displays, featuring various ceebs in action: Maria Piñata walking through shallow surf or giggling at a party, Mikhael Kustov pacing a tight-rope between two tall buildings, scenes of Andrew Collins starring in the book *Octo-man's Revenge*, Janet Eisenhower singing "What a Woman Wants" while cavorting amidst a host of werewolves and vampires. Whatever was being shown on the screen changed with breathtaking frequency, rarely holding on to one perspective for more than a half a second.

The screens and their contents were not unlike what Tommy remembered from his own apartment, not unlike what they were in a billion other apartments around the globe. But right now, he didn't want to see them; right now, they bothered him immensely. He wanted to read his paper-book, but was unable to. With his fatigued mind and inability to concentrate, his reading skills were just too poor. He would read part of a sentence, his mind would drift, and then he would start the same sentence again. Sometimes he would read two or three paragraphs, and then realize that he had only skimmed words; no images were in his head. At these times, he wished that he could be watching a real book, and then he'd reproach himself because he realized that that was precisely what Shripton wanted.

And then one day (or night, as he had no idea which), he woke up. That is, he woke up on his own, without a blueshirt there to take him to room E544. For a moment, he lay still on his back, looking at the white ceiling, not sure where he was. He turned to his right, and saw Guan Cierno on the screen, attempting a free-ascent scaling of the Dawn Wall of Yosemite's El Capitan in the United States, with a voice-over relaying his thoughts.

A voice-over. He was hearing the voice-over as if he were at home. Clear as crystal; no background noise. The machine sounds and the ticks and hums were gone.

He felt like he was floating in a pool of sunshine.

He fell asleep again, watching Guan Cierno negotiate a particularly tricky section of the vertical rockface.

*

"You look well-rested, Tommy. I'm not sure you're ready to go out there quarterbacking or whatever it is you do, but I would say you managed this stage of your recovery quite well."

Tommy grimaced.

Shripton opened a drawer and took out two tumblers and a bottle of Scotch, setting them deliberately on his desk in front of him. "I know last time you were disinclined to join me, but this time I hope you will partake." He poured some amber liquid into each tumbler and took one for himself. Tommy considered for a few seconds, and then took hold of the second. Shripton smiled, raising his glass to Tommy before taking a sip. Tommy again waited briefly, and finally took a sip himself. He grimaced again, this time unintentionally, as he felt the liquid burn his throat with surprising intensity.

"Now what?" he said.

"Now? Now we just wait until you are ready to reconnect to the Hive."

"Your PRADIT brainwashing sessions didn't work. If you are going to reconnect me, you will have to kill me first." He hadn't meant to say that; it came out as if by its own volition, but he was rested and feeling antagonistic and buoyed with confidence.

Shripton smiled again. "Nobody's going to kill you, Tommy. When you are ready, you will reconnect yourself. Nobody will do it for you."

"Do you always talk in riddles? I still don't see where any of this is going."

"Look at your left forearm."

Tommy did so, at first with the palm down, then slowly turning his hand until the palm faced upward.

"You see those three marks?"

There were three greyish dots on the skin, along a line, equally spaced about 3 centimetres apart. He had noticed them early in his imprisonment, but, other than the regularity of position there had been nothing distinguishable about them, and he had dismissed them as curious blemishes. Now he regarded them more intently.

"When you want to connect to the Hive, simply press the three points simultaneously." Shripton demonstrated, pushing the first three fingers of his right hand, spread apart, into the fabric of the red unitop that covered the flesh of his left forearm. "As simple as that. Whenever you are ready."

*

Some things changed in his routine, and some things didn't. He still spent most of his time in the limited confines of his room, with the three screens, which never stopped showing various ceebs and compelling images. He tried to avoid looking at them, focusing as best he could on his paper-book. He was no longer given food in his room; a blueshirt took him to a cafeteria for his meals. The cafeteria room featured a counter, upon which were stacks of plates and various pots and metal containers of food. Behind the counter was a pair of swinging doors, presumably leading to the cooking area. The bulk of the room was occupied by half a dozen rectangular tables, each with eight seats. Tommy thought of the mess tent of the Ketchen, similar to this in many ways, except here the walls were solid and white instead of brown fabric and the floor was tile instead of dirt and grass.

Among other things, these meals gave him some perspective of time. With the even illumination in his room unchanging, no view of an outside world where a sun would rise and set, and no chronometer of any sort, time had become a fluid with no fixed points, like a deep ocean with no light. With the meals, however, there was now an established pattern in time: a cycle of three. Breakfast, lunch, and dinner. A daily routine.

But the biggest surprise was that he was not alone when he had his meals. At any particular time, there might be a dozen blueshirts sitting at the various tables, both male and female, most with no insignia but some with black bars over the left breast. Occasionally he would recognize one of them from room E544 or as a guard who had accompanied him. They would invariably smile at him and say, "Hello, Mr. Antikagamac." Sometimes there were green-uniformed individuals. He never saw a red unitop there; in fact, Shripton was the only person he'd ever seen with red.

Quite distinct from the blueshirts and the greenshirts were seven individuals wearing white, loose-fitting beltless and pocketless pants and loose white shirts, four buttons down the front. Just like what Tommy was wearing.

The Freemen.

The first time he walked into the cafeteria, there they were at one of the tables: Harrison, Ameline, Lennox, Hans, Karl, Benoit. And Frenna.

Seven.

No Myles. Who were the others that were missing? He couldn't remember. They gave their lives, and he couldn't even remember who they were.

But the rest: he wanted to run up to them and embrace them. Hug Frenna. Shake Harrison's hand, grab Lennox by the shoulders. Tell Ameline he could still find the volume of a cone. Tell them all that he had survived, that he had been tortured, and now it was over.

But he didn't. Their faces stopped him. If they were surprised to see him, it was apparent only from a little flicker in Lennox's eyes. Or Frenna's faint smile.

Their faces were shadows and hollows, softened and stretched by fatigue and hopelessness like melting wax masks. Harrison's hard eyes burned at him like coal. *He still thinks I betrayed them,* Tommy realized.

The blueshirt who had accompanied Tommy tapped him on the shoulder and indicated the counter. "Help yourself," he said, and proceeded to do so himself. Tommy followed, and filled his tray with cold pea and basil soup, an open-faced cucumber sandwich, two roast beef sandwiches with horseradish, and tea. He took the tray to the one open seat at the table of Freemen, sitting opposite Hans.

Lennox was the first to speak.

"We were wondering what had happened to you."

The Freemen, Tommy found out after several awkward attempts at conversation, had been subjected to a different "treatment" protocol than Tommy's. All their meals had been here in this cafeteria, and they had been forced to meet each day with Annetta Briscotte, a woman who introduced herself as a former Ketchen who now embraced the society of the Hive. (At the first meeting, Ameline attacked her with the goal of gouging her face with her nails, but was subdued by a shot from an electric pistol.) They were held two to a room or three to a room. But similar to Tommy, they were subjected to the pleasures of room E544. Similar to Tommy, they were awoken at irregular intervals, never allowed to complete a full sleep. Similar to Tommy, the electronic music with its ticks and hums and discordant sounds was ever-present in their rooms.

But unlike Tommy, these parts of the "treatment" were continuing.

Early on Harrison and Ameline had commenced a hunger strike, but that only resulted in them being forced to watch their confreres subjected to level-45 shocks. End of hunger strike.

None of them had ever heard of Edgar Cornelius Shripton, and Frenna's quick glimpse when he was with Tommy that time in the corridor was the only occasion any of them had seen a red unitop on anyone.

They all expected Tommy, now that he was there, to explain to them what this "treatment" was all about, and what the future held in store. But Tommy, of course, knew no more than they. "Some sort of brainwashing mechanism," was all he could offer. "They're trying to break us down, and when there's nothing left, we will embrace their 'Hive' because we have nothing to hold onto."

"Then why have they stopped your torture?" Karl asked accusingly. Tommy realized that they weren't convinced that he had used the word "*us*" properly.

He shook his head. "I don't know," he said softly, looking at his tray. He had not yet begun eating. Now he picked up one of the sandwiches and took a bite. The rest of the table was silent. Conversations could be heard among the blueshirts at the other tables; laughter broke out among a group of five at the table across from Tommy.

Without warning, Ameline stood up and threw a bowl from her tray, smashing it against a wall. Instantly, she crumpled, and Tommy saw the blueshirt at the door with the electric pistol in his hand. Two other blueshirts were picking Ameline up from the floor and dragging her semi-conscious from the room. Harrison had leapt to his feet, but there was nothing he could do. All the conversation in the room had stopped and the blueshirts in the room either looked at Ameline being dragged out or at the table of Ketchen. Slowly, they returned to their eating and their conversations. One of them got up and began to clean up the pieces of the smashed bowl.

"It's hardest on her," Lennox said quietly to Tommy, referring to Ameline. "Remember, she has a child back home."

4

"You are not the same as the Ketchen," Shripton replied. "Of course your treatment will be different. They have never been part of the Hive. I can't tell you much more because the uncertainty they are experiencing is part of the treatment protocol. What I can tell you is that it works. Without any physical damage, it is effective with a success rate of over 90%, and typically within eight months. You don't have to worry about your friends."

Tommy stopped in his tracks. He and Shripton were walking along the corridor of the twelfth floor. *Eight months!* "You bastards! Eight months of torture. Anybody would agree to anything after that. You and I have very different views of success!"

Shripton was waving his hand. "It's not eight months of torture. Look, I shouldn't have said anything. The treatment is complex. And the end result is truly in their best interests . . ."

Tommy snorted derisively.

". . . and that goes for you too. You can't see it now, but in time you will."

"I still don't understand this whole sick game. If being part of the Hive is so bloody good, then why not just connect us and be done with it? Do it, and then we'll say, 'Hey, Shripton! You were right! Thank you!' Because it's all a bunch of bullshit, isn't it?"

"It's more complicated than you think. Ah! Here we are." The door slid into the wall with a *ffftt,* and the two of them, followed by a blueshirt, entered a large room: a fitness facility. It was small compared to most of the facilities that Tommy had used in the past, but nevertheless it seemed to have a reasonable assortment of exercise contraptions, and Tommy recognized the usual attachments to measure things like oxygen consumption rate, lactic acid concentration, heart stroke volume, and so on. Two women were in the room, one using a power squatting machine and another a running simulation apparatus. Both stopped immediately when they saw Shripton and Tommy.

"Good day, Ms. Evans. Good day, Ms. Stevens. I assume you recognize Mr. Tommy Pierre Antikagamac."

The two women disengaged themselves and came hurrying. "Good day, sir," they both said to Shripton, but their eyes were all for Tommy.

"Mr. TeePee," one said, putting forth her hand for Tommy to shake. Tommy instinctively took it, but didn't say anything.

"The Knights are the bloody pits without you," the second added, also putting out her hand. "Sanders couldn't hit Mazurski's fat ass from 20 yards if it had a bullseye!"

"Excuse us, ladies," Shripton said with an annoyed tone.

The two women stepped away as if they had been slapped. "Sorry, sir," they said to Shripton. "Mr. Antikagamac," the second one said to Tommy. The first one just nodded. She was red as a beet.

Shripton led Tommy to a bench that ran the length of one of the walls of the room. The wall behind the bench was haphazardly decorated with posters depicting featureless silhouettes performing various exercises. *Posters*, Tommy noted, *not screens with moving images of well-proportioned ceebs.* The other three walls were mirrored, making the room look much larger than it really was.

"You will want to utilize these facilities if you want to keep yourself fit for American football," Shripton was saying.

"I have no intention of playing football."

"Well, that's nothing you have to worry about right now. Still, this room is at your disposal for use whenever you want."

"What is this place?" Tommy asked, exasperated. "This . . ." he waved his hands vaguely to indicate the whole building and not just the fitness room . . . "place? This whatever? Who are you people? You keep answering me in riddles. Why are you not connected? Why does nobody know about this 'institution'? What do you do here? I just . . . I just don't get this! Any of it!"

Shripton took a deep breath, almost a sigh. "What do we do here? You know, Tommy, sometimes I'm not even sure. If you want a name, it's the Institute of Security. We like to call ourselves TheBusiness. Our mandate is the protection of the Hive. To do so, we work behind the scenes, as it were. There you have the answers to two of your questions. To protect the Hive, we have to operate outside of it. We are a specially trained lot, and we look after an organism that unites 8 billion people. When we are off duty, we are part of the Hive, just like everyone else. But when we are on duty, we disconnect. We have that ability. Anyone connected trying to enter this building is stopped, so the only ones who are inside are members of TheBusiness. If anyone connects from inside this building, and sometimes we have to for various reasons, electronic shielding prevents any outgoing thoughts.

"To outsiders, this is the P. B. Stoddard Building, P. B. Stoddard Inc. being a nondescript mid-level technology supplier and trader that, of course, does not exist. When we come on duty and disconnect, a computer simulator seamlessly takes over our wavecode. My wife thinks I buy and sell chip adapters for Pentagon PlayPorts. She thinks it is the most boring job in the world. When I leave here and become reconnected, any incoming probes related to my day at work are intercepted and routed to the simulator. And of course, I've had sufficient training that I will not inadvertently send any thoughts relating to what happens here."

Tommy was astonished. And as confused as ever. The people here, the blueshirts, the greenshirts, Shripton – they lived both in and out of the Hive! He put his hands over his eyes. Then a sudden thought occurred. A revelation. "Oh, you bastard," he said, screwing up his face, "you want me to join you, don't you! You're recruiting me! You want me to become part of TheBusiness!"

Shripton laughed before he could stop himself. "No, no! I . . . I didn't explain . . . I didn't mean to lead you to that conclusion. No, you're not going to become part of this racket. You're going to rejoin the Hive, and hopefully recover your career in American football."

Tommy shook his head and turned to look at the two women working out in the room, each of them trying hard not to glance over in his direction.

"So to that end, as I said before, this room is for your use whenever you want it. Just tell your attendant, and he will accompany you."

My attendant. You mean the pistol-toting guard stationed outside my door. One of the women was pulling on a rowing simulator. *Timing is all off,* Tommy noted absently. *Legs should drive first, into the back, finish with the arms.* For the briefest of moments, he wondered why she didn't access a coach or a rowing professional. He even considered sending her his vision of the technique. Then he remembered his circumstances, and admonished himself for his Hive-like thought. It had been a while since he had had such.

He felt glum. "If you're not recruiting me, then what's all this about? What are you doing with me? Why did you cause the glitch that separated me from the Hive in the first place? You still haven't explained that! You just say, '*We had to do it.*' Nothing makes any sense!"

There was a desk with a monitor and a chair at the corner of the room adjacent to the bench on which they were sitting; Shripton went and took the chair, then placed it in front of Tommy. For the next minute or so, he tried rather comically to balance the chair on one of its legs, correcting and be-balancing it each time it started to tip. Tommy watched annoyed, and finally said, "What are you doing?"

"You try. You're an athlete. I'm sure you'll do better at this than me."

Tommy didn't react. Shripton set the chair back on its four legs and sat down on the bench. "Simple physics. If the centre of mass of the chair is stationary in a vertical line above its base of support, it will stay balanced. But the base, as it were, of a chair on one leg is exceedingly small. As soon as the centre of mass strays outside the vertical line above the base, it falls," he finished, as if that was all the explanation that was needed.

"Instability," Shripton replied to Tommy's silence as if he were giving away an answer to a quiz. "A chair on one leg is inherently unstable."

"And if I hit myself on the head with a hammer, it hurts. So what?"

"The Hive is the greatest feat of social engineering in the history of humanity. And yet it is inherently unstable. *Inherently* unstable. It's like the chair on one leg. It needs a touch of correction on occasion to keep it balanced. That's what we do. TheBusiness. We provide those minor corrections to keep the Hive balanced. As long as we do so, the Hive will survive and thrive as far as can be seen into the future. But without corrections, it would collapse, deceptively slowly at first, and then cataclysmically."

"You're talking riddles again."

"Let me get specific. Let me talk about the world's best player in the world's most popular sport. Cross-over appeal to a startling variety of people. A ceeb with the largest number of followers in the history of the Hive. That's you, of course. People the world over access your thoughts on your football opponents, your pre-game ruminations, your girlfriends, the ceebs you follow – did you know that Janet Eisenhower was the number 14 most accessed musician before you began following her, within days of which she became number one? – your favourite screen games . . . Twelve year-old girls in Ecuador who don't know an American football from a pumpkin know that you like to dance the lep-hoza. In fact, the lep-hoza wasn't a craze before you started doing it. The day before you left to do your training in the Fallowlands, 122 million people knew that you had kippers, sausages, and tea for breakfast."

"Yeah, yeah, I know all that. So what?"

"Cromby's Axiom. Celebrity begets more celebrity. The more followers a ceeb has, the more buzz is created, and that attracts even more followers. To give a somewhat dark analogy, it is like sharks being attracted to the blood of other sharks in a feeding frenzy. Of course, it's not bad like that, and a 'saturation point' is typically reached at which followers simply re-distribute themselves, like a wave that breaks or a pyramid of sand which collapses. For example, Gina Cardelli the actress – my wife buys all the same clothes that she wears; drives me nuts – Gina Cardelli recently became the number one accessed ceeb. Our computers calculate that she will peak at 255 million primary followers in 17 days, which is just over 3%; 60 days after that she will be down to number 20. Simple redistribution.

"Computer simulations show that this continual cycle of saturation and redistribution is healthy for the Hive, and, in fact, the Hive can continue in all its pointless glory forever. There is no fundamental restraint on that 'saturation point,' however. It can be arbitrarily high. And that is where the problem comes in. The inherent instability of the Hive. Through quasi-random processes, the saturation point will – not '*might*,' Tommy, but '*will*' – reach a dangerous level, a level at which the ceeb, whoever he or she is, will upset the precarious balance of the Hive *before* the safety valve of redistribution takes place. And the Hive will collapse.

"You remember, of course, Waomi Holan. Surfer, actress, tall and gorgeous – she rocketed to number one status, reaching 12%. Cromby's Axiom. Calculations predicted saturation at 54%. She had that . . . something, charisma, I don't know, that appeal that just seemed to hit the right spot for people. Of course, like everyone else, she had certain personality flaws. Nothing dangerous at her level, and in fact nothing significant that she or anyone else was even remotely aware of. But had she reached 28% and her hidden dislike for Blacks leaked out, the Hive would have become infected. At 32%, it would not have been containable."

Tommy snorted derisively. "So we're all lucky she drowned."

"Regrettable, but true. Had she reached 32%, our society would have collapsed chaotically. There's Akima Ballulu, remember him?"

"That crazy skateboarding guy, the world champion who refused to compete at the Olympics?"

"And named world's sexiest man, although I didn't see it. Tremendously popular. Saturation would not have been reached before 27%. It wasn't his outsized lifestyle that was dangerous. It was the fact that Akima believed in God. Behind the persona, he was actually a good citizen; he never sent any religious thoughts to anybody, never gave any outward signs. In fact, at the height of his popularity, very few people knew. Nevertheless, religion is a particularly aggressive malady; Hive infection would have occurred at 21%. It had to be stopped."

"What happened to him?"

"Knee pain ended his skateboarding. With that small change, saturation occurred at 8%. Akimo's a happy man today."

Knee pain that was not even real. Tommy was shaken as he considered the insidious reach of The Business. And then, in an instant, he felt a clammy sweat break on his brow. *Waomi Holan drowned in heavy surf off Hawaii.* Shit la merde!

"What about me? Where do I fit in? I was no threat to this 'health of the Hive.'"

"No? Consider: Your rate of sending and accessing thoughts during waking hours was 1.4 standard deviations below the mean value for the population of the Hive. That in itself is nothing dangerous, but it's one of many indicators of a disquieting bent you have towards unhealthy individualism. Look at how quickly you turned antagonistic to the Hive. My word, that was startling! But that was you. Few others would have reacted so extremely. Your little group's idea that a month with Europe disconnected from the Mother would result in a revolution?" He shook his head. "No. A few people would have turned rogue, but not many.

"No, Tommy, the danger to the Hive was *you*. Your thoughts, deeper than even you were aware. The revolution that you had hoped would come with your sabotage is very similar to what might have actually happened had your popularity continued to grow. Your saturation level was predicted to be 72%. Seventy-two percent, Tommy. Do you realize what that means? Do you realize how dangerous you were? The wrong thought . . ."

"So what's the story? You plan to kill me? Or destroy my career?"

"No, no, no. You might have been killed, of course; Harrison almost did that work for us. But, no, nobody's going to kill you. And I certainly hope, as do others here," – he nodded towards the woman who was now running on the resistance treadmill – "that you will once again incite hundreds of millions to watch you throw an oblong ball for great deals of money."

"So I'm back to where I started, Shripton! What are you doing to me? I'm not *still* dangerous? Where is all this going!"

"Be patient, Tommy. Trust me: you're going to be fine. Now, I'm sorry, but I have a meeting I have to attend. I'll invite you to my office again very soon, and we will continue this conversation. Now I'm serious: use this facility. It will do you good. You still look like a mountain, but you've probably lost a great deal of strength in the last few months. You'll feel better, I'm sure."

A blueshirt slipped quietly into the room when Shripton left, but Tommy didn't notice. He was visualizing Waomi Holan in a bikini during a California surfing competition years earlier, all legs and almond eyes and flowing hair, standing on the board as firmly as if she were standing on the floor in front of him. Dead in a "surfing accident." He closed his eyes and shivered.

5

After four days, he was taken back to E544. As his arms were attached to the overhead cables, he felt a weight of despair as heavy as a moon. He'd thought it was over. He was crushed.

He closed his eyes and braced himself. Then a pain as intense as anything he'd ever experienced ripped through his lower right abdomen. His knees gave way, and he hung from his arms. When he looked, he expected to see his stomach ripped open and his guts spilling onto the floor, and was distantly surprised to see that his shirt was white and not red with blood.

"Level 55, Mr. Antikagamac."

Level 55. With effort, Tommy gathered his legs beneath him and stood weakly. Then an identical bolt of pain shot through his lower left abdomen.

This time, when he had regained his legs, the shackles slipped from his wrists and ankles and receded back to the ceiling and floor. Two blueshirts supported him as they returned him to his room.

*

He lay on his bed with his arm over his eyes. The jennix was showing a ceeb who called herself Colonel Wendi, a singer-dancer who always performed semi-naked and painted head to foot with luminescent colours. Ten thousand fans danced in front of her, many doing the lep-hoza, writhing under strobe lights flashing blue and red and green.

Baby wanna shine
Baby gotta whine
What's ya doin', always makin' me droolin'
Heart's on fire, oh yeah yeah yeah, baby . . .

Tommy tried not to hear the lyrics, just like he tried hard not to see the images that relentlessly poured day and night from the screen. Just like he was trying not to think. But he had to think, didn't he? Where was this going? What was the purpose of fighting all . . . all this?

Abruptly he rolled off the bed and went to the door, which opened automatically.

"I want to see Shripton," he said to the blueshirt there.

"I'm afraid Mr. Shripton isn't here, Mr. Antikagamac. It's 2:00 a.m.; he'll be here in seven hours. Can I help you?"

"No." He went back into his room and sank miserably onto his bed.

*

He dozed; he woke up with two blueshirts standing beside him. Once again, he was taken to E544. He was again given two jolts at level 55, one on his right elbow and one on his left shoulder blade, each one feeling as if he had been stabbed with a red-hot chain saw. He was half dragged back to his room and left seated on the edge of his bed.

In his mind, he was looking at heavy surf breaking off the coast of Hawaii. Empty. The ocean was empty. No Waomi Holan; the girl had drowned. TheBusiness. "*Level 100 will kill you.*" Was that his fate? "*Nobody's going to kill you, Tommy. When you are ready, you will reconnect yourself.*"

Level 55. He felt cold; he pulled the blanket from either side of him and wrapped it over his shoulders. His forehead was damp with clammy sweat. They were going to do it again. He wasn't sure if he could take it. Maybe it will be level 60. And then level 65. They would do it until he broke. Or until it killed him. Waomi Holan. He saw Frenna, her look of defiance. The other Ketchen. "*A success rate of over 90%, and typically within eight months.*" Where was the future? What was he holding on to?

He pushed up his sleeve, looked at the three little marks on his left forearm. Despair overwhelmed him like crashing surf. He spread the first three fingers on his right hand, and then simultaneously pushed them into the three marks.

And nothing happened.

*

"You don't want to be back in the Hive, Tommy. You want to be finished with the treatment, which is quite understandable, but that's very different. If you're honest with yourself, you'll realize that. You are not ready to be reconnected, and both of us know that."

"Honest? You have the nerve to say *honest*? You told me I could reconnect any time I wanted to. You said it was my decision. In short: you lied, so don't tell me anything about 'honest.'"

"I must apologize for my verbal shortcomings. The nuances of thought are so subtle that language is often a clumsy means of expression. It's like trying to pick up a particular grain of sand on a beach with a shovel, isn't it? Language? Direct non-verbal communication, of course, doesn't require this spoken interface, and so misunderstandings don't tend to happen in the Hive.

"It's fascinating when you think about it. Can you imagine how much miscommunication has happened in the history of humankind as a result of the inadequacy, the coarseness, of language? Just think how many marriages have broken up because husband and wife talked in parallel streams past each other, and even though they were practically aligned in their thinking, they just couldn't make their thoughts clear to one another. Hah! Think how many unfortunate marriages came to be for the same reason! What about business deals? Wars? Questions of ethics? It seems language is very good with black and white, and can even name colours like blue or 'burnt umber' . . ."

"Will you cut the bullshit, Shripton?"

"But it is interesting to speculate, is it not, how the world would have developed had the Hive always existed? It certainly would have been less interesting, along with being less bloody. Now to our present misunderstanding: 'Wanting to re-attach to the Hive' is not the same as 'putting an end to present circumstances.' Your action was the result of the latter, not the former. You are still not yet ready."

"Shit, Shripton, I'm never going to be ready! I don't know what you want from me! I give up; I'll do anything you ask. What more is there? Should I start staring at my screen, pretend I'm enjoying Maria Piñata and Colonel Wendi and Andrew Collins? Is that it? If that's it, I'll do it, because that hell's a whole lot preferable to level fucking 55."

Shripton contemplated for a moment, then rose from his chair and went to the bookcase. He followed his finger with his eyes as he scanned across the books on one level and then on another. He seemed to be searching for a particular volume.

"And why do you have paper-books?" Tommy asked petulantly.

"Quite illegal," Shripton answered. "But, like you, I find them immensely satisfying. It takes work to read one, of course; even if they were legal, I don't think they would catch on in the Hive. Ah, here we are. *A Compendium of Short Fiction.* I think you'll enjoy short stories. These are by masters of the written word, from times when the written word had masters. Nowadays, there are no masters, of course; personally, I find the books of the Hive so much drivel packaged in a kaleidoscope. Each new blockbuster outdoes the previous one only in the profligacy of its image and sound technology. Even books that remake the stories of paper-books lose the soul of the original, exchanging it for simple sensory actuation. Books stimulate the periphery of the mind, Tommy, but paper-books stimulate its depth. Which I suppose is why paper-books became first unpopular and then in time illegal.

"Some of these might be a bit tricky for you to read. What I will do is check off a few that I think you'll enjoy."

"Why are you giving me stuff to read? I thought you wanted me to join the Hive; you should be extolling the virtues of real books as opposed to paper-books, shouldn't you?"

"If I'm not going to say what I believe, then there's no reason for you to trust me, is there?"

"I don't trust you anyway."

"Hopefully I can change that." Sitting at his desk once more, Shripton opened the book to the index and, taking a pen, checked off the titles of a half a dozen short stories. "At any rate, I think you'll enjoy these. I certainly did."

And so, Tommy returned to his room with a paper-book in his hand and as much confusion as ever in his aching head. Yes, his headache was back, he realized. A news story featuring Angela Merriweather and her recent breakup with Hans Kreichwald was on the jennix. He sat and pressed the palms of his hands into his eyes. That's when he realized that someone had greatly reduced the volume of sound accompanying the visual from the jennix. So that he would find it easier to read his paper-book.

"You're trying to drive me insane, aren't you?" he said aloud. "When I finally lose my mind, that's when I'll be ready. That's it, isn't it? That's when you will reconnect me?" He was trying to decide whether to embrace his coming insanity or resist it when the door opened. "E544?" he said morosely to the blueshirt.

"Sorry, Mr. Antikagamac."

He felt sweat burst from his armpits. For a brief moment, he visualized driving the heel of his hand into the chin of the guard, knocking him cold and seizing the electric pistol from his belt even as he collapsed to the floor, then firing and demobilizing the two others at the door before they had time to react, then racing down the corridor to freedom . . . But of course, only the first of those actions would be successful, he knew. His shoulders drooped as he allowed himself to be led out.

Shackled by his wrists and ankles in E544, he felt his legs quivering as he awaited the first bolt of pain. *Will it be level 55 again? Or will they increase it still higher?* He felt a buzzing on his left quad, reminiscent of the electro-stim therapy he sometimes had for minor injuries.

"That was level 5, Mr. Antikagamac."

A buzz again, this time on his neck. Level 5 once more.

A sting behind his knee, like the snap of a wet towel against his flesh. "Ow!" he said.

"Level 10."

The shackles released themselves after a dozen jolts of level 5 or level 10. His elation was such that he almost laughed.

On the way back, he again visualized his sudden vicious assault on the blueshirts accompanying him. It was to no purpose, but he found himself smiling, in the way that a daydream of a pretty girl you don't know could make you smile. In the Hive, of course, such a daydream was never yours alone. In the Hive, a visualization of a vicious assault would result in a hundred helpful therapies crammed into your skull within minutes.

Back in his room, he made the decision to fight Mr. Edgar Cornelius Shripton. He would resist the inevitable insanity, at least for now. He balled up two shreds of toilet paper and stuffed them in his ears. He could hardly hear the announcer's voice as his jennix showed the London Knights getting set to kick off to the Barcelona Rams. Tommy turned his chair so that he faced away from the screen, and opened up *Treasure Island*. He still had a chapter to read in the paper-book.

Later he would go to the exercise facility to train his atrophied muscles.

◊

❝You are a fascinating study, Mr. Antikagamac. You were the darling of the Hive, rich beyond measure, at the top of your sport, essentially the embodiment of everything 8 billion people strive for. Yet two months of disconnection, and you are as antagonistic to the Hive as any Ketchen. Your 'conversion,' if I can call it that, was far more extreme than I had expected. I suspect that reading a paper-book had more than a little to do with it, but I am still surprised."

"I'd say *you* are a fascinating study. You're not attached, so you know exactly how I feel. Free. Free to think whatever I want and know that my thoughts are mine alone. Free to imagine on my own, and not have the image given to me. It's an incredible feeling, and I'd been robbed of that my whole life! I can multiply 12 times 17 and *I* come up with the answer, not a computer. You must know what that means! How that feels! I'd look up at the night sky without star charts and ephemerides and see stars, planets, the Milky Way, meteors, and for the first time, they were naked, beautiful. You understand! How can you not? I saw satellites drifting across the night sky, and I hated them because they were intruders. I hated them for what they represented. You see all this too. You and the other people in this institute or whatever it is. I'd think you'd want to *join* us, not destroy us!

"And you just smile! What do you say? What makes you so different from me?"

"Actually, I'm not very different at all."

Shripton wiped his sweaty brow with the towel that was around his neck. The two of them were side-by-side on cycling apparatuses in the fitness room. About two weeks had passed since Tommy had received level 55. In the intervening time, he'd seen Shripton a half-dozen times, usually in the latter's nineteenth-floor office. The discussions were light, often philosophical, with Shripton doing most of the talking.

"That is, if you ignore the fact that you are twice my size and, according to the readout, your oxygen uptake is about three times mine. And that's not a smile, it's a grimace. I haven't been on one of these things for half a year. I've gained 3 pounds since my wife agreed that I would lose 15.

"No, our main difference is perspective. You see the Hive as a malevolent entity that has sprung upon humanity and now holds us, blind and weak, in its evil clutches. Am I right?"

Tommy shrugged. "You're going to say it wasn't sprung upon us; it sprung from within us. Yeah, I know, I know. And your job is to save us from ourselves, to keep us from descending into the black pit of misunderstanding and war. I'd do the same if I were in your shoes. I get the sales pitch. Well, bullshit."

"That's not bad, Tommy, except for the expletive and the heavy reliance on sarcasm. I might yet make a philosopher of you. Nevertheless, it's incorrect. It didn't 'spring' at all. As you know from your history, the Hive simply evolved. In every step in its development, from the days of metal electronics and hand-held interfaces to skin graft technology to aural and visual implants and finally to seamless thought communication, the same pattern was followed: technology is developed, a vanguard establishes its use, meek voices raise issues of privacy and ethics, which simply get swamped in the global rush to embrace this newest step in humanity's glorious march to the future.

"The point is, every step in the development of the Hive has been accepted as desirable. Nothing was imposed upon us. Year after year, item by item, technology upon technology: people *chose* to have more complete connection with each other, *chose* to have less privacy, and *chose* to expose deviant thought patterns. Then you have D'Alembert's principles: "In a world of quasi-infinite numbers there are no unique thoughts," and "Honesty obviates the fear of oversight." Privacy is no big deal, in other words. The Hive is simply the logical and inevitable culmination of human development. It's what people want, Tommy. If you took the Hive away, history would repeat: the Hive would either redevelop, or war would destroy the world. Most likely, the latter. We were very lucky the first time."

"You sound very cynical."

"I am. I've told you before: it's one of my worst traits. But it comes back to what I'm saying about perspective: I see the Hive for what it is, and if I'm cynical it's because it disappoints me. Humanity has traded Aristotle and Nietzsche for Ru Finn and Jeannette D'Alembert, Bach and Mozart for Janet Eisenhower and Colonel Wendi. Edmond Hillary is just a quaint figure from our more primitive past, because 80 million people watch Uzaki Ming and others climb Everest in less than five hours as part of the This Games or the That Games. The average IQ of the top hundred scientists is ten points higher than a similar group 50 years ago, which is also the length of time since a human has been further away than lower Earth orbit. A century ago, science promised us Martian colonies; it delivered to us Insta-Splink and Sensup."

"So we used to be much better off, before the Hive."

"No, no, no, no, no. Not at all. My cynicism is my own. My opinions, which people complain that I extol too often inside these walls, are quite unpopular, even among other members of TheBusiness. Even those who read paper-books well prefer the 5-second philosophical thoughts of Ru Finn to hours poring over the abstruse and often irrelevant writings of Descartes. People think I'm crazy because I prefer the paper-book of *Crime and Punishment* to the real book, which lasts two hours and won three Lizzi awards. No, in a different time, I would have been the weak hand trying to hold back the flood."

"So why do you do what you do? You should be on my side! You should be with me and the Freemen!"

"No, you're missing the point. As I said, I see the Hive for what it is. It disappoints me because I find its society shallow and its imagination stifled. But that's me. Others with similar perspective to mine, in fact *most* others, would quite disagree. And in reality, who cares? There's no particular purpose for humanity in the first place. Which brings us back to your crazy statement: were we once better off? That's a joke. The history of humanity is essentially the history of war. Brutal, bloody, absurd. It seems war is the bane of intellectual species. And since the threat of annihilation scales with technology, as long as there is war, global destruction is inevitable. As I said, we were very fortunate to have survived the last one. We wouldn't survive another. Well, the Hive has taken war away from us. I don't have to explain that to you; you've been taught that since you were old enough to understand what war is.

"Then there is our planet, our woebegone Mother Earth. Not to be confused with the Mother. A paradise of nature she was, beautiful, subtle, ever-changing, a jewel of a planet. For eons she developed and nurtured and harboured life in its splendid myriad manifestations. And then mankind came along: a disease, a sickness, a parasitic infestation. If Mother Earth could have done so, she would have vomited the human race out into the void. But she couldn't, and the humans made her sick. I mentioned dreams men once had of conquering space, of colonizing Mars, of travelling to the stars . . . What a tragedy if that had happened or would happen! Imagine: the blight of humankind infecting the rest of the galaxy like some kind of metastasizing cancer. Ah, what good fortune for D'Alembert's fifth – or is it her sixth? – principle: "Every civilization will destroy itself before it can develop the technology for star travel." Which explains, of course, why Earth has never hosted visitors from other planets, but that's a different subject. Back to the Hive: we are still a parasite, but no longer one that will kill its host. We are no longer a danger to the Earth and to the Universe.

"So why do I do what I do? You have your answer. The Hive is the success story of human evolution. I work to protect it."

"No, that's still not right," Tommy said. "I'm not an intellectual / philosopher / historian, but I know in my gut that it's not right. And even if it was to some extent, what's wrong with leaving the Freemen alone? Or me? Why not allow people to leave the Hive if they want?"

"You know the answer to that. Everyone does. Humans are inherently dishonest. In the days before the Hive, nobody was ever sure what was true and what was false. Before the Mother, nobody knew if the information they were given or the images they received were true or tainted. And security? Let's not forget what you were trying to do before you were taken here. That was no real danger, of course, because it was a controlled situation for us. But had it not been controlled . . . It's not a trivial point you are raising; the privacy versus security debate was huge, absolutely huge in the months leading up to the decree making connection mandatory. As you know, people around the world chose democratically and overwhelmingly in favour of security.

"As for the Ketchen, they're quite incapable of doing any serious harm, and in fact, their existence is desirable."

"What do you mean?"

"It's healthy to have an enemy. It brings people together. It supports patriotism. Blah, blah, blah, the idea that 'out there' are outlaws, bad guys who want to do your side in. If the Ketchen didn't exist, we'd probably invent them. That's why we don't bother to eradicate them, which could actually be done quite easily."

"So why do you persecute them? Capture them? Torture them?"

"First of all, we need to ensure that they remain incapable of doing harm, so we can't just let them develop willy-nilly. We have to keep groups isolated, prevent them from developing means of serious destruction, et cetera, et cetera. Secondly, we have to keep their numbers viable. The only places they can live are the Fallowlands, which would obviously cease to be what they are if any sort of significant population existed. Their circumstances certainly inhibit significant procreation; nevertheless, we need to keep their numbers stable.

"Thirdly, if you have an enemy, it's good to have the good guys win from time to time. Capturing Ketchen, and then allowing them into the Hive, gives people a sense that the Hive is both a powerful and benevolent entity. Again, it's a matter of good health. As to torture, I agree that the PRADIT is unpleasant, but it's not torture. And its benefits are wonderful. Once in the Hive, former Ketchen are invariably grateful to be part of it. They are honestly happy. Of course, the PRADIT part, in fact, everything associated with TheBusiness, is hidden from the Hive.

"Unfortunately, the majority of Ketchen brought into the Hive are not from our doing; they're random captures, resulting from inevitable chance contacts. Forced attachment to a resistive Ketchen without the PRADIT is far *more* unpleasant, as well as being dangerous. Thirty percent suffer psychological damage, and a third of these require extermination."

"Extermination," Tommy repeated sourly. "They're not a bunch of rats."

"I know, Tommy. Look, we're trying to do the best we can for your friends. If you can think of something different, let me know."

"Yeah, I can think of something different: bring them back to where you took them, let them go. And me too!"

"They're better off here, Tommy. And you too. You'll see."

"Bullshit."

They pedalled in silence for a few moments. "Ah, God!" Shripton exclaimed, wiping his brow again with his towel. "Five minutes still to go! How can people do this?"

"I thought you didn't believe in God."

"I don't *believe* in Him, but I do *invent* Him from time to time in order to curse."

7

The lot of the Freemen had not improved. Oh, their meals were regular, and they were taken to the fitness room and forced to exercise for an hour each day. They also had 90 minutes of "free" time in a recreation room, which included a variety of interfaces and simulator screens allowing the user to hit a golf ball, throw a football, or swing a baseball bat at a Steve Serensen pitch. Each day they had instruction and "practical tips" for entering life in the Hive, and sometimes they were brought to a theatre to watch a 3-D fulsense adaptation of a popular book ("but it's so much better when you experience the *actual* book in your mind!").

None of these things was optional.

The rest of the time, they were confined to their rooms. A screen on the wall showed wonderful 3-D images of laughing and smiling and active people from all over the world, often with a backdrop of a dramatic vista, accompanied by pleasant and soothing music. Then the screen would go blank and the music would be replaced by the mind-grating electronic sounds that had so irritated Tommy. This happened randomly, day and night, although the only indication of "day" and "night" was the schedule of the meals. The illumination in the room never changed.

Sometimes once, sometimes three times a night, each would be brought to room E544.

. . . effective with a success rate of over 90%, and typically within eight months.

. . . Once in the Hive, former Ketchen are invariably grateful to be part of it.

. . 'Dear Felix: Happy eleventh birthday. Mama.'

. . . "It's hardest on her. Remember, she has a child back home."

"Shit la merde," Tommy said to himself.

*

"I've figured out your game."

"Really?" Shripton struck the ball with his putter and grimaced as it stopped 90 centimetres to the right of his target. "I didn't know I had a game, but go ahead."

"It's me for them, isn't it?"

"You'll need to elaborate a little."

Tommy stood by the doorway inside Shripton's office like a grizzly bear on its hind legs. "It doesn't make any sense, but what does around here? I'm ready now. You wanted me to find a reason to join the Hive, and it's been staring me in the face all along. The Freemen. A simple deal: I re-attach to the Mother, and you let them go. I agree to never even *dream* an independent thought, I play football again, I become the world's number one proponent of the virtues of the Hive. I'll be your inside man; I'll keep that chair from tipping over. And I keep that up for the rest of my life, because if I screw up, I know you'll grab my friends again. You know how much I'm giving up. This is what you meant by me being ready:

that I be willing to give everything up for the others. I'm willing to pay that price, so it's clear I'm ready now to join the Hive."

"You're right." Shripton leaned over his putter again. "It doesn't make any sense." He stroked the ball, and this time it rolled directly into the cup. He beamed in satisfaction.

"But I'm right . . ."

"What? No. Listen, would you be so kind as to take my photograph?"

"What?"

Shripton pulled open the bottom drawer of his desk, and after a moment's rummaging, he stood up with a small plastic device in his hand. "Here. This is a camera."

Tommy's confusion was all over his face as Shripton gave him the camera. It was like a small black box, dwarfed in Tommy's hand.

"Look through here, do you see? When I tell you, just press the button on top."

Shripton took his putter and stood proudly beside the ball in its cup. "Can you see the ball?"

Tommy shook his head no. "I can't see anything."

"You're looking at the wrong place. Move your head back a bit. Now, do you see me? Make sure you can see the ball and the top of my head. Good? Now press the button. It's on the top. That's it."

Shripton took the camera back and examined it. "Here," he said, showing Tommy the device. There, on a tiny 2-D screen, was a slightly skewed image of Shripton holding his club. He replaced the camera in the drawer.

"I'm going to attach. I want your guarantee that you will bring the Freemen back to their home." Tommy rolled up the left sleeve of his loose white shirt, and keeping his eyes on Shripton, he spread the three fingers of his right hand.

"Not going to work." Shripton casually turned and replaced the putter in the rack on the wall. "You can press if you want, but nothing will happen. There is an override to the circuit."

Tommy pressed anyway; nothing happened. "Fuck!" he exclaimed.

"You rarely used that word in the past. Is that something you picked up from the Ketchen?"

"I'm so sick of this. I don't know how to get out of this nightmare!"

"Be patient, Tommy . . ."

"Oh, screw your patience, Shripton! All you ever say is 'be patient,' 'when you're ready,' and all that horse-manure. Make a bloody decision: either do it or don't do it. I'm as ready as I'm ever going to get. Hell, I'm getting less ready every day. You're *making* me less ready! You're making me go through this PRADIT crap or whatever it is to try to soften my brain so that I'll somehow magically want to join the Hive, but then you give me illegal paper-books to read so that I don't have to spend my time staring at the garbage on my screen! You paint a picture of the Hive as this bloated, self-important, purposeless entity, and that's supposed to convince me that I should become attached to it? I mean: what the hell?"

"First of all, Tommy, I'm not trying to sell you anything. Even if I tried, it would be ineffective, wouldn't it? I want to make sure that you are fully aware of your feelings towards the Hive. Nothing hidden, from me or from *yourself*. Look: you and I perceive certain shortcomings of the Hive, so let's not pretend that we don't. These are our opinions, and we're welcome to have them. I'm being totally honest with you, and I hope you recognize that.

"As for paper-books, and doing what I can to reduce the sound volume in your quarters, I'm just trying to make your stay a little less unpleasant. Others here might disagree, but personally, I think its effect on the PRADIT is quite minimal."

"If you are being so honest, then tell me when I get out of here."

"I don't know, Tommy." Shripton paused before continuing. "It might be a long time."

Tommy said nothing. He didn't know what else to say, what else to ask. He put his hands over his eyes and stared at the orange lines between his fingers where light filtered through the skin.

"Come. Let's go for a walk. When was the last time you saw the sun?"

It took a second for the words to filter through the morass that was his mind. The sun? He hadn't seen the sun since he'd been trapped in this cage. How long was it now: months? Years?

It felt like years. It felt like everything else in his life had happened eons ago. In reality, it was about five or six weeks, he knew. Nevertheless, it had been long enough for him to forget what he was missing. He tried to keep his expression sombre; he was still angry and frustrated, and he wanted to keep Shripton aware of that, but the offer to see the outdoors was like a starving man being offered bread.

He followed Shripton, and of course, two blueshirts silently followed him. Tommy was becoming more familiar with the complex layout of crisscrossing corridors on the various floors of the building, but still found them confusing. He could only guess at the work being done inside the offices that they passed, some with closed doors, others with doors opened to reveal men or women working in front of wall-sized image consoles or desktop interfaces, sometimes alone, sometimes in groups of three or four. Most were blue, a few were green, and some wore unitops that were a muted dark yellow colour.

They stepped to the side as they passed a greenshirt moving a cabinet with a hydrolicart. "Good morning, sir!" the greenshirt said snappily.

"Good morning, Evan," Shripton answered. "Glad to hear your father is doing better."

"Thank you, sir."

"Good day, sir," a blueshirt said, one whose bosom strained at the material conspicuously, reminding Tommy achingly of something else he hadn't seen in a long time.

"Sally," Shripton said, nodding pleasantly.

Shripton stopped at one of the open office doors. "Good morning, Oliver," he said to the blueshirt standing at the console inside. Four black bars on his breast, Tommy noticed.

"Ah, good morning, Mr. Shripton."

"You haven't forgotten our little wager of last Sunday?"

"How could I, with you reminding me every day this week. Don't worry. You'll get your Scotch. Good morning, Mr. Antikagamac."

Tommy inadvertently nodded back, quite sure he had never seen the man before.

At the elevator, two greenshirts stepped out, saying, "Sir!" in unison.

"Gentlemen," Shripton answered politely.

They stepped into the vacated elevator, Tommy and Shripton and the accompanying blueshirts. "Sixteen!" Tommy said before anyone else had a chance to say anything. Nothing happened.

Shripton laughed lightly. "Anything special about floor 16?" he asked.

"Just trying."

"Your voice profile isn't registered." Shripton turned to the closed elevator door. "Twenty-three."

A one-second *whoosh!* and the door slid open.

Tommy followed Shripton (followed by the two blueshirts). There was much less activity on this floor, although they did pass one door through which Tommy saw a half-dozen yellowshirts seated in front of a wall interface.

They stopped at an undesignated plain door with a tiny window. Shripton pushed it open, revealing a stairwell. They climbed 15 stairs to a small landing and another door. Shripton had to give two pushes before he finally budged this one open, and Tommy immediately felt the caress of cool, fresh air. He closed his eyes and sucked it in.

"Bullocks!" he heard Shripton say.

Tommy opened his eyes and stepped through the doorway.

"The sun was shining an hour ago."

They were on the roof. The sudden sense of height and openness constricted Tommy's throat, and with a gasp he stepped back.

The door opened onto a concrete platform about 4 metres square and 30 centimetres high, with a railing on one side. The structure that held the door sat like a box behind it. Tommy stood at the threshold, half in and half out, gripping the railing with his left hand with all his might. He knew the two blueshirts were behind him, waiting for him to proceed. *Just give me time*, he thought. He forced a deep breath, then took two short steps along the platform, never relinquishing that grip.

A chill wind brought goosebumps to his forearms under his loose shirt. Iron clouds drifted humourlessly across the sky. Shripton had already stepped from the platform onto the vaster expanse of the roof itself and was walking around helter-skelter, gesticulating at the sky and the surrounding buildings.

". . . one of the shortest buildings, as you can see. This is the front of the building, squeezed in as we are. Out there is Queen Elizabeth II Square. On the other side, over here . . ."

Tommy was barely listening. On one hand, he was enjoying the air, the cold breeze (*What month is this? Must be December* . . .), but on the other, he was keenly aware that he was 24 floors above street level.

Maintaining his hold on the railing, he looked slowly around. This was London, his home, although beyond QEII Square and the Churchill Complex, 60- and 100-storey high-rises blocked his view. For the briefest of moments, he tried to ingress MapView, then immediately rebuked himself for falling back upon his old habits. It was happening more and more frequently, and he didn't like it.

I must be looking south, he figured. The Thames flowed murkily over there somewhere, the Old City would be off to his right a few kilometres, and in the unseen distance beyond a dozen rows of these high-rises was the new region that replaced the huge swath of the city that had been destroyed in the war.

". . . so the Stoddard Building essentially has eight sides. Come on, Tommy, I want to show you my garden."

Tommy clung to where he was.

On either side from his location, east and west, the roof was bordered by the sides of taller buildings. The one on the east side was about three storeys taller, and a metal ladder attached to the wall rose vertically from his roof to the higher one. On the west side, behind the box of the doorway, a much taller building loomed, perhaps 20 stories higher. On the north side, opposite QEII Square, the taller buildings stopped and his building, the Stoddard, spread out of his sightline behind them. Here and there, ventilation hoods squatted. A half-dozen large needle antennae poked up 10 and 15 and 20 metres, and there was also a fenced-in area featuring a rather complex assortment of rods and electrical boxes, the nature of which Tommy couldn't even guess.

"Don't be afraid. The roof is quite solid, believe me. You don't have to go close to the edge. I wouldn't have brought you here if I didn't think you could do it."

Shripton was only 5 metres away, in the direction away from the street. Absolutely no reason not to at least step that far.

Tommy stepped off the platform and let go of the railing. He stood for a moment to feel the security of his stance and his traction before moving farther.

"Good." Shripton was standing beside a rectangular enclosure, raised knee level above the rest of the roof. Inside was mostly brown earth, although here and there were a couple of sad green bushes.

"This is it. There's not much growing at this time of year, of course. This one here is one of my favourites; it's a rhododendron and gives great colours in late spring. That bush is weigela, and over there: believe it or not, I planted that *Pinus mugo mughus* as a seedling the size of my hand three years ago, and see how well it has taken. I cleaned everything else up over a month ago, ready for next spring. I guess I prefer annuals to perennials because I like something different each year. And they're easy. But I use most of the space for vegetables. This whole area here I grow tomato plants, this area is beans, and over here I plant peppers. Ah, I grew cucumbers for the first time last year, and I had about six or seven that were this big" – he held his hands 20 centimetres apart – "and tasted like a dream.

"So that's my garden. I try to put at least a few minutes into it each day during the growing season. I keep a chair here too. Summer's too hot, and fall is usually too windy, but spring is a marvellous time to sit in the sunshine by my garden and read a paper-book, even if it's only for a few minutes. I never seem to have enough time to do that."

A gust of cold air made Tommy shiver. The temperature was about 4 degrees, he figured. But it wasn't from just the cold that he shivered. He felt relatively safe next to the garden, far from the edges of the roof; nevertheless, there was nothing, *nothing* at those edges to prevent him from sliding off should he slip or stop him being blown off should he lose his balance or . . . What if the blueshirts tried to push him over the edge? What if that was Shripton's reason for bringing him here: to . . . He moved back to the railing and gripped it tightly.

Shripton came along beside him. "That's about how much time my wife gives me when I talk to her about my garden too. Let's get back in: it's chilly. Sorry about the sun."

*

Later that day, Tommy was lying on his 2.5-metre bed with his hands over his eyes, blocking off the incessant light from the ceiling. A voice from the screen droned in the background, something about an underwater swimming record. Tommy wasn't listening. In his mind, he was lying on his back in Switzerland, and he was looking up at a leafy canopy. The sun was up there somewhere, beyond the leaves. A soft breeze touched his cheeks.

It was dark under his hands, and his fingers were wet. For the third time since he'd lost the connection, he was quietly shedding tears.

*

"Ahhh! Shit!"

"Level 40, Mr. Antikagamac."

Tommy stared at the paper-book in front of him, but he wasn't reading. He couldn't concentrate. He was tired to his bones, but he didn't want to lie down. He was trying to hold up, to *not give in*, to keep his sanity. Nocturnal trips to E544 had resumed, and he wasn't sleeping regularly. Sometimes he was zapped with level 5, sometimes with level 40. The uncertainty ate into his mind like worms. He wasn't sure if he could take it much longer.

Don't give in, don't give in, don't give in . . .

*

"I want to see Shripton."

"I'm afraid he's not here."

"When will he be back?"

"He's taking Festive Day holidays. Maybe in a couple of weeks. Can I help you?"

"No." Tommy turned back sullenly into his room. "What's the date?"

"December 21."

The door closed behind him, and he flopped onto his bed face downward. *Festive Day holidays. I'm getting bloody level 40, and he's showing me his garden and taking Festive Day holidays.*

The thought came to him with the suddenness and clarity of a lightning stroke. What Shripton was trying to do.

He put his hands beside his head, still face down. "Shit la merde!" he said into the pillow. Then he sat up, his eyes wild. "Oh shit la merde shit la merde shit la merde!" He dropped back down onto his back and laughed at the ceiling. "Oh, Shripton, you conniving spawn of a sow! You conniving spawn of a SOW!" He jumped up and began pacing. "Have to think, have to think!" Soon he realized that the room was too small for his thoughts.

"I'm going to work out," he told blueshirt at the door. "Take me to the gym."

*

MERRY FESTIVAL in red letters on squares of shiny green paper strung to the wall greeted staff members, Ketchen, and Tommy when they entered the cafeteria. There was *HO-HO-HO* in gold letters, arcs of red ribbon, and an artificial evergreen tree in the corner decorated with red baubles and silver tinsel and a red-coated Father Festival perched at the top. Tommy, as usual, filled his tray at the counter with twice the amount of anybody else, and went to sit in the empty seat at the end of the table where the seven Freemen were already eating. Their mood was perceptibly sulky, again as usual, and conversation among them was infrequent and muted. Typical dinnertime hubbub from two dozen people at the other tables drowned their silence. The two blueshirts at the door were telling jokes to each other.

Tommy stared down onto his plate and carved a piece of ham. "We're breaking out of here," he said with a voice so low that the only person who could hear was Ameline, seated beside him.

Ameline dropped her fork. She retrieved it hastily, as if the floor were on fire. Staring down at her plate, she whispered, "*Quoi?*" with a shallow breath.

Tommy took a mouthful, then continued. "I know how to get out of this place. I know how to escape." He took a drink, then looked down again. "It's a long shot; perhaps some time you can work out the mathematical odds."

"How!" Her hushed voice was so intense it sounded angry.

"In time. Can't talk much. Tell the others."

Ameline quietly said something in French to Lennox beside her. By now, everyone at the table had sensed that something significant was happening, and eating and conversation had conspicuously ceased. Tommy saw some blueshirts glance at their table.

Ameline reached and took Harrison's plate from across the table. "These potatoes taste like shit!" she said aloud, scooping some of her mashed potatoes onto his plate. The other Freemen got the message, and conversation accompanied by excessively noisy eating quickly drowned out the whispers as they were passed around. Tommy felt the hard eyes of the others boring into him. He kept his head down and ate quickly.

"This building isn't designed as a prison," he said quietly to Ameline. "It isn't operated as a prison. I know how to beat it. I can get us onto the roof, and from there, we can escape. I have a plan. But I can't tell you everything now." He looked up and saw the blueshirt looking at him. He took Ameline's plate and emptied her uneaten green beans onto his.

"I'll tell you bit by bit, a little at each meal. Let someone different sit beside me each time so that it doesn't look suspicious. Pass the information on whenever you get a chance. Just be careful. We have time; we're going to do it in10 days." He looked up at Hans, who was eyeing him from the far end of the table. "I'm forgetting my German," he said conversationally. "*Eins, zwei, drei . . .* What comes next?"

*

Over the next several days, Tommy conveyed, in bits and pieces, his plan for escape. To the others, its premise was unconvincing, the details ludicrously vague, and its chance for success preposterously small. It was a frustrating mechanism for clarifying and debating, this whispering of fragments of thoughts between mouthfuls of food and sentences of faked unrelated conversation. But it was the only opportunity available.

He spoke at different times with Harrison, Ameline, Lennox, and Frenna.

"Harrison doesn't trust you," Lennox said.

"Does he have a choice?"

"I think we all have the same misgivings. It's not really you, per se, that we don't trust. It's a) you're a bit delusional, and that's not a criticism because it would be quite understandable given this madhouse, or b) if you're not delusional, then we think you're being played for a fool by this Shripton character."

"No! Damn it, this is frustrating! There's too much to explain. I can't argue here. You just have to take my word. Harrison too. Everybody. I'm not delusional. I'm not a pawn. Shripton *wants* me to escape. What he *doesn't* want is for all you to come with me – *that* he isn't expecting."

"But why would he want you to escape? I still don't understand."

"It's complicated, Lennox. I can't explain it all now."

"They tracked us through you before."

"It won't happen this time. They have no attachment to me unless I agree to let them."

"That's what your Shripton says . . . You must realize, Tommy, how absurd all of this sounds."

"As I said, do you have a choice?"

"That's why we're listening . . ."

*

"*Alors.* You know we are on the fourth floor. Frenna and me, we are in 421. That's easy; it's the fourth prime number over 400. We are in sight of the elevator. The others are around the corner. Harrison and Hans are in 442. Lennox, Karl, and Benoit are in 446. Twenty-one times four divided by two gives 42. And plus four gives 46. So all you have to remember is the number four. The doors open automatically from the outside. From the inside, we have to press a button to get someone to open it for us. If there was a fire, we would be cooked.

"Hans says the electric pistol shock varies as one over the distance cubed, with a 4-metre attenuation feature to prevent it from killing people if they are too close. What that means is that it will paralyze you if you are closer than 4 metres, but at 8 metres it will only be a very painful shock. At 12 metres it won't stop anyone.

"At night, there are always two in the blue uniforms in front of the rooms with the men. They are usually sitting at a table, playing cards. There is a woman who sits in a chair outside my room. I hear cleaners in the corridor every night at the same time; Karl made a water clock with drips in his WC – did you know that? – and he says they come two hours after we return from our evening bullshit.

"That's everything I know.

"Eh! Bouge-toi!" she said irritably, pushing Hans, who had just put his elbow on the table beside her.

"Monsieur TeePee, get me out of here."

*

"I'm stronger than I look. I may not be able to walk, but believe me, I will buy you some time. I'll take out two of them with these." Frenna nudged her crutches.

"You're coming with us."

"No, don't be stupid. All I will do is slow you all down. You'll never escape with me. So there's nothing for me to lose by staying behind, but there's a great deal for me to gain. If I can crack the skull of one or two of these sadists, if I can know that somehow I've helped you and the others to get out of here, I will die one very happy woman."

"You're not going to die, and you're getting out of here with the rest of us."

"Come now, Tommy, you aren't being realistic. Without me, you have very little hope of success, but at least there is hope. With me, you have none. And if you don't escape from this place, you have none. So don't make me responsible for your failure. Let me be a factor in your success. Get them out of here. Give Ameline some hope. Please. I can't walk. But I can fight."

"You don't have to walk. I'm going to carry you."

"Don't be silly."

"I'm not silly. You know, you don't weigh a whole lot more than my football equipment. And with you on my back, I can still run faster than Lennox. Don't waste your breath arguing. We're not leaving you behind. We're not leaving anybody behind."

*

"So we escape. Even if we do, it means screw-all. You just say, 'I'll take care of you.' I'm sorry, but that's not enough. We're in the heart of a city of 15 million people, and the nearest fallowland is way the fuck up north in Scotland. We're going to magically make it out of London and then another 500 kilometres without food and dressed like fucking inmates without anyone even noticing that we're not connected to them?"

"We're not going to Scotland."

"Of course not. We're going to swim to Canada."

"You're going to Switzerland. Home."

Harrison didn't say anything, but Tommy could tell that the Freeman was caught off guard.

"There's a tube station three minutes from here. Huge crowd in the Square and nearby, which works to our advantage. Noise and confusion and people carousing with friends and watching the New Year's Eve fireworks. We're all dressed the same way; people, if they notice us, will just think we've partied too much. Unlikely anybody will try to ingress us. My thumbprint – Biometric Elite. Any transport in the world. I'm allowed a solo carriage. Advantage of being a top ceeb. The network can take us right to the coast. Same thing there: chunnel train leaves every half hour at night. My thumbprint gets a solo carriage car for me and my entourage. Perk of the elite class.

"At Calais, I put you on a train to Besançon. That's the best I can do; from there, you have about 50 kilometres to the border of the European Fallowlands."

"They'll track you. You have that thing in your head, and they'll track you. Or you'll be recognized. Shit's sake, how can you *not* be recognized? You're six-foot-eight. They'll find you and then we're all toast."

"I'm not going with you."

Harrison turned and looked directly at Tommy. Tommy saw a blueshirt at the door glance in their direction.

"Tell him," Tommy said aloud to Karl, startling him. "Tell Harrison I was the one who found the chanterelles."

"It's true," Karl said with his German accent, not knowing what he was talking about.

Harrison looked back at his plate. "What happens to you?"

Tommy took a few seconds before answering. "I get captured. I get re-attached."

Harrison stopped eating.

"The train will get you to Besançon in about three hours. I'll hide out at least that long. Then I'm going to try to make my way to Paris. If I don't make it, that's okay, but I want to make as big a splash as possible."

"Splash?"

"I'm dangerous to the Hive. Shripton said so himself. I have too many bad ideas, and too many followers. That's why I'm being kept here. TheBusiness wants me under wraps, until I've lost my 'independent tendencies,' until I'm no longer dangerous.

"Think about it: When I'm 'found,' it will be the biggest news story in years. Within minutes, *Luker* will have me all over the world. I'll be forced to reconnect, of course; there's no way TheBusiness can step in and prevent it or control it. In fact, I'll be totally *out* of control. And once I'm connected, everyone will know about this place. And everybody will know my thoughts about what I've come to feel since I left the Hive. It will be a shocking story. Everyone will wonder how I could have gone so wrong, how I could have let myself get brainwashed by the evil Ketchen. I'll be a pariah. I'll be public enemy number one. But my thoughts will be out there. And the point is: I'm not just some inconspicuous demented drone. I am Tommy Pierre Antikagamac, the best player on the best team in the world's most popular sport, and my thoughts will be more than a fart in the breeze. Cromby's Axiom. The chair will be tipped.

"What you guys hoped to do with your sabotage? It's going to happen after all."

"But you'll be reconnected."

"It's going to happen anyway. It's just a matter of time. Might as well do it on my terms."

"Well, I appreciate your magnanimity, but this all sounds a bit much. I have to agree with Lennox. He thinks you're deluding yourself. You're reading into this Shripton character a whole lot that doesn't exist . . ."

"Aw, come on! I'm not making this up! He's the one who showed me how to escape!"

"Do you know how many things can go wrong? Do you have any idea what the chances are of even a *tenth* of this working? You manage to beat and disarm six guards, without a soul hearing you, and then you come and find out you can't even open our doors!"

"Maybe I'm hoping for a bunch of sixes. You have a better idea?"

*

Of course, Harrison was right. So many things to go wrong.

Tommy was staring at the illuminating ceiling of his room, a featureless white glow. Sound of Elyssa Motari's cooing voice came from everywhere as she danced on the screen to Tommy's right. On the other wall was a 3-D picture of Guan Cierno scaling El Capitan, viewed from afar, a spot with nothing but flat vertical rock all around, his limbs splayed like an insect. *I'd like to have ingressed his thoughts at that time,* Tommy thought absently, then shook his head and chided himself. *Too tired,* he thought. *So damned tired. I've been tired for months.*

Harrison was right.

But Shripton wouldn't be having him do this unless he knew it was possible.

He'd have to climb that ladder. He'd have to get out on the roof, with Frenna on his back, and climb another three storeys' height. It was *that* thought, more than the ceiling illumination, more than the sounds from the screen, even more than the uncertainty of his next trip to E544, that kept him awake and staring into the light.

It was easy, he told himself. The weight of Frenna was no problem; in fact, the physical act of climbing the ladder was an impediment of the most trivial nature. He could do that as easily as most people could run up a flight of stairs. So why the fear? The fact that he was high above the ground made absolutely no difference in the physical task. The terror of the height was illogical. *Totally illogical. I just have to not think, just do it. Just one time. Twenty seconds, and we're at the roof entrance into the next building, a building with no blueshirts or greenshirts or any such people; in fact, a building that would be quite empty New Year's Eve night.*

That roof entrance had to exist, or else Shripton wouldn't have shown him the ladder.

Just one time. Twenty seconds. A few steps, an easy climb, and we're there.

If I don't do it, the Freemen are lost.

Think positively. I will do it. I will. I will just blank my mind for 20 seconds. Frenna, I'm going to get you back to your books. Ameline. Lennox. You're going home. Harrison.

I wish I could go with you.

He was still awake when the door slid open.

"I'm sorry, Mr. Antikagamac," said the blueshirt.

The poster image on his wall showed two fizzing glasses of champagne clinking together.

Tommy had asked to go to the gym an hour after supper just to hide the fact that he couldn't stop sweating. Now here he was, pacing his room again. Sit down, try to read. Pointless. The words were all over the place. Get up, lie on the bed. He hummed along with Janet Eisenhower, who was singing while she waded ankle-deep in green water by a white sandy shore. An old man dressed as Father Time and carrying a sickle was following her comically. He got up and began pacing again.

He thought about goats. In particular, he thought about the goat he'd tussled with when he'd been starving. In theory, it was a simple matter of killing the animal and he would be fed; in practice, in the physical reality of the situation, he'd chickened out. He wondered if something similar was about to transpire. Would he be able to carry through with what he had to do?

It was 43 minutes until midnight, according to an old-fashioned clock that was placed anachronistically at a corner of the screen. It was the first time since Tommy had been captured that he knew the time.

The screen was showing crowds of revellers somewhere, maybe London, maybe Lisbon, maybe Oslo . . . Still 43 minutes until midnight. Why was time going so slowly? He wrung his hands. They were sweaty. Forty-two minutes until midnight.

He waited agonizingly as the long minute hand on the clock face crept slowly around the bottom of its arc. "Crazy, these old clocks," he said to himself. More ceebs, More revellers. More fireworks.

Fifteen minutes before midnight was the right time, he'd decided earlier that evening when he'd seen the clockface on his screen.

At 11:44, he decided he couldn't wait any longer. He felt himself hyperventilating; he took three purposeful deep breaths. Then he pressed the green button beside the doorway.

A blueshirt opened the door almost immediately.

"I want to go to the gymnasium," Tommy said.

"Uh, sure," the blueshirt said uncertainly. "Are you okay? You look sick." He glanced at the other blueshirt, who was standing a couple of metres away.

"I'm fine. I was just doing some push-ups," is what Tommy should have said, but the thought didn't come to him. In fact, nothing particularly intelligent came into his mind; all he saw was the blueshirt stepping away, hand drifting towards the electric pistol at his hip.

Dammit, they know! they know! they know! Tommy's head was screaming. In panic, his fist flew out, a punch to the head of the blueshirt nearest him. In an instant, he had the arm of the second, wrenching it back, and as the head came forward, he brought up his knee and smashed it into the blueshirt's face.

A second had gone by, and there were two men crumpled on the floor. Tommy was breathing as if he had just completed a series of wind sprints.

Are they dead? Oh, please, no, don't let them be dead. Tommy stood frozen in place as he stared at the bodies. Outside the context of his sport, he'd never struck a man in his life. And now there were two that he might have killed. *Oh shit. Ohshitohshitohshitohshit.*

The second body made a noise. An arm moved.

Tommy snapped out of his trance. With his huge hands, he grabbed hold of the ankles of both the blueshirts and dragged them through the open door into his room. He removed the pistols from each of their holsters, and then took the communication devices that were attached to each of their belts. The one who had moved pushed at Tommy weakly with his arms, saying, "What? What?" as he became semi-conscious. Tommy stepped outside and pressed a red button, closing the door and leaving the blueshirts locked inside.

The corridor was empty. A screen that the guards had been watching showed a ceeb named Lester Thomson, an action book actor, speaking to the camera in front of throngs of revellers. It was 14 minutes to midnight. Tommy saw blood on the floor at his feet. He dropped the two communication devices, ran down the corridor, turned left, and found the door that led to the stairway.

One flight up. He gave up trying to hold two pistols in one hand; he left one on the stairs. He pushed open the door and stepped out quietly.

He was in a small nub of hallway just off a corridor, similar to his own floor. Assuming everything else was the same, 442 and 446 would be to the right.

He peered around the corner. Sure enough, there was a table located about two-thirds of the way to the far end, maybe 15 metres away, but instead of playing cards, the two blueshirts were sitting back in chairs watching the screen in front of them. Tommy hesitated a moment to collect himself, and then he was sprinting towards the table. With his rapid and enormous strides, he was upon the blueshirts before they knew what was happening. From 2 metres away he pulled the trigger on his pistol, and one of the guards dropped before he was able to stand, knocking over the chair as he fell. He immediately aimed at the other and pulled the trigger, but nothing happened. He pulled again, again nothing. By this time, the second blueshirt was standing, hand already on his pistol, but Tommy was just too fast. Dropping his useless pistol, the big man was upon the guard in an eyeblink, grabbing the wrist with an iron grip and delivering a palm that simultaneously broke the man's jaw and knocked him unconscious.

Already, it was becoming easier.

But there had been too much noise. As quickly as he could, he took the communicators and the pistols from the two guards, the first of whom was groaning and trying weakly to get to his knees, and then Tommy sprinted silently to the end of this section of the corridor, where it made a T with the main section of the floor. The elevators were to the left.

"Mickey?" came a female voice from the other direction. "What are you guys doing? It's not even midnight!"

Tommy looked around the corner, and only a handful of steps away was the source of the voice. She reached for her pistol instantly, but Tommy had already leapt towards her and pulled the trigger on his.

Even as she was crumpling, Tommy took hold of her and slung her over his shoulder, then ran back to where the others were on the ground. One was still unconscious. *I hope he's not dead,*

Tommy thought, but this time without any hesitation in his move-ment. The other was on his hands and knees, still dazed.

Tommy pressed the green button outside 442 and then the one outside 446. The doors slid open, and instantly the Ketchen were there, helping Tommy carry and drag the guards inside. Then they pressed the red buttons, and the doors shut.

"That one doesn't work," Tommy said to Hans, who was picking up one of the pistols from the floor. "I shot it once, then the second time it was dead."

"The capacitor has to recharge," Hans said, shaking his head at Tommy's ignorance. "Three seconds."

"Let's go," Harrison was saying, already hurrying down the corridor.

Tommy caught up and then ran ahead, turning right at the T and racing to room 421. He pressed the green button, and Ameline and Frenna practically spilled into the corridor, the latter bound-ing forward on her crutches.

"Give me those," Tommy ordered, squatting so that she could climb onto his back.

"This is absurd," Frenna protested. "I'm just going to slow you down!"

"Frenna!" Harrison barked. "Get on his back!"

With Frenna clinging around his neck, Tommy ran ahead and the others followed. Down the corridor, then left, then right. Through the door and into the stairwell.

Less than three minutes had passed since he'd left his room. "This is bloody working!" he said aloud without realizing it.

"How far?" Lennox was asking with a hoarse whisper.

"Nineteen flights of stairs from here," Tommy answered quietly.

"Let's go! Stop fucking around!" Harrison croaked, even as he began running up the stairs.

The others hurried behind, their steps on the metal stairs ringing hollowly. Tommy didn't like the noise, but then figured it made no difference at this point. Nothing to do about it anyway. He followed last, with Frenna on his back, gliding up silently. He held the crutches in his right hand, and with his left, he pulled on the railing to assist his climb. Between the ninth and tenth floors, he passed a labouring Lennox, and shortly after that, he passed Hans and then Ameline. His own legs were burning, and he wasn't sure he could make it without a stop to rest.

Fifteen. Sixteen. Seventeen. Six flights to go. He tripped, pitching forward. Frenna shrieked. Tommy caught himself with his hands, absorbing his and Frenna's momentum with his open left hand and with the knuckles of the right that held the crutches, instantly splitting open the skin. He took a second to wince against the pain, and then he continued upward. Between 18 and 19 he passed Karl and Benoit, who had been reduced by fatigue to walking. "Hurry," Tommy tried to say as he passed them, but it came out "Hu-ee." At the twentieth floor, he realized his left hand was hurting as much as his bleeding right knuckles; his palm bore an angry red welt from where he'd arrested his fall on the stairs.

He reached the top simultaneously with Harrison, who immediately doubled over and vomited. Tommy stepped past him onto the landing in front of the door to the roof and knelt, allowing Frenna to step from his back to the floor. She stood on her good leg, holding the railing as Tommy passed her the crutches. "Tommy," she said quietly. "I don't know what will happen from here, but for all this, I want to say, 'Well done, my son.'"

Karl and Benoit dragged themselves up a few moments later. Harrison was still doubled over. In time, Ameline arrived; she bent over beside Harrison and put her arm over his shoulder as together they stared into his vomit. He spat one more time, then abruptly stood up. "Where the hell are the others? Shit!"

They heard shuffling a short distance below, and then Hans dragged himself into view. "Thank Gott!" he said when he saw that he was near the top.

"That leaves Lennox," Benoit said.

"Fuck," Harrison muttered, and he began to make his way down the stairs.

"No," Tommy said, recovered enough now to have regained his senses. "You stay here. I'll be faster." And with that, he ran back down the stairs.

He found Lennox four floors below, leaning over the railing and wheezing noisily. Tommy threw him over his shoulders in a fireman's carry and proceeded to run back up. But just as he got to floor 23, the highest floor of the building before the 15 steps up to the roof level, the door burst open.

The blueshirt was as surprised to see Tommy right there as the latter was surprised to see him, and in the split second it took the blueshirt to shout, "They're right here!" Tommy had smitten him unconscious. The guard's hand was on his pistol, but he hadn't had time to draw it from its holster. Lennox, meanwhile, had fallen from Tommy's shoulder, but was recovered enough to land safely though awkwardly.

Tommy grabbed the handle of the door and pulled to keep it closed. "Run!" he called to the others. "I'll hold the door here!"

"Are you a fucking idiot?" Harrison shouted. "Where are we going to go without you?"

"Jam the door!" Ameline cried. She pulled a crutch from under Frenna's arm and ran down the stairs to Tommy.

The handle on the stairwell side of the door was the type that was a horizontal metal bar that acted as a lever when you pushed it. She shoved the crutch between the handle and the door, with the two ends of the crutch lodged against the doorframe. At that instant, the door was pulled from the other side, then pulled more vigorously. The crutch held.

"Let's go!"

Tommy felt coolness on his face; Harrison had pushed open the door to the roof. Tommy and Ameline ran back up the stairs while the others hurried through the door. Tommy stopped to pick up Frenna.

"No," she said. "I can only slow you down. You hurry. Save the others. Get them to the Fallowlands. I'll get you some time." She wielded her remaining crutch.

"Don't force me to get violent with you," Tommy answered as he squatted down beside her. "I've already punched too many people today."

"Please, Frenna. Hurry!" Ameline said. "I'm not going anywhere without you!"

Frenna took hold of Tommy's shoulders and mounted his back. "You're a dear."

It was dark and rainy. Tommy felt gusts of wind even before he came to the doorway. He hesitated. This was it. All he had to do was *NOT THINK* for about 30 seconds, and then it would all be over.

He stepped out onto the roof.

Rain pelted onto his face like cold needles. The wind was a roar in his ears. He felt light-headed. Like he might fall. Fall and tip over sideways, fall off the edge of the roof, all those storeys down . . . down . . .

"Oh shit," he said to himself. "Shitshitshitshitshit. I can't do this! I can't! Oh shitshitshitshitshit!"

Was it the wind that was roaring, or the crowd? Queen Elizabeth II Square. Look at all the people, so tiny, so tiny so far below . . . Why did it have to be windy? And dark? And wet?

He was too tall, the wind too strong. He was going to tip over. Maybe he could just go on his hands and knees, close to the gravel on at his feet . . .

No! He had to hurry! Frenna depended on him. So did the others. He heard them calling him. It wasn't far. The others did it. He could do it. *Come on, lean away from the edge. Lean into the wind. There. That's more stable, isn't it?* He took a step. Another. Another. *Not far now. Just a few more steps. Where? Where is the ladder? Shitshitshitshitshit! WHERE IS IT! Don't panic. It's just there.* He ran five steps, grabbed hold of the metal ladder, and sank to his knees.

Made it. The first part. He clung to the ladder like he was clinging to his life. He was hardly aware of the weight of the woman on his back; he knew she was shouting something – *"Hurry! Hurry!"* – but first he had to control his breathing. He looked up. The ladder latched on to the side of the taller building like a metal caterpillar. Straight up. Straight, straight, straight up. Forty rungs? Fifty rungs? Rain pelted his face, blurred his vision. Harrison was leaning over the top, yelling something. He needed time. *Just, just give me time.*

But of course, there was no time. *How long for the blueshirts to go down one floor and run up the extra flight to the roof? They'd be here any moment.*

Forty rungs. He could climb that in 15 seconds. *Just do it and it's over!*

He stepped on the first rung. The second. The third. Then he stopped, paralyzed by his terror. He stared straight ahead at the wall 30 centimetres from his face. Decorative style brick and mortar. Frenna, on his back, was screaming.

"Just look up," he told himself. "Not left, not right, not down. Just up. That's all." *Take a step. Reach, grab the next rung. Hold it with all your might. Take a step. Reach, grab the next rung.* His neck quivered from the mental effort he was exerting to focus every bit of his attention on the next horizontal bar of steel just above his eyes. *Hold it with all your might. Take a . . .*

There was a brilliant flash of light, followed by a *boom!* which vibrated through his chest. He shrieked and pulled himself tight against the ladder. Another flash, another explosion.

Fireworks.

He wasn't strong enough to keep his head from turning, looking. The crowd in Queen Elizabeth II Square, far below. Far *far* below, just beyond the edge of the roof from which he'd been climbing. And he was far above that edge, suspended in mid-air. Height upon height. He was in space, one wet slip from falling . . . falling . . . His eyes were like saucers. He couldn't shut them, couldn't look away. He sucked in air in a gasp of horror. The wind blew, and despite his strength, he felt that he was on the verge of losing his grip on the wet rungs. He was sobbing like a baby, he knew, but he didn't care. He had to get his feet onto something solid. He had to get *closer to the ground!*

"Tommy! Tommy!" Was that Frenna? Yes, it was Frenna. "Tommy!" Or Harrison. He thought he heard Harrison's voice. "Tommy! Tommy!" He was on the roof. He was low, as low as he could get. Stable. Squatting low, hands touching the gravel surface. "Tommy!" He thought he heard Ameline's voice, far away. Nice voice. "Tommy!" He'd never told her how much he liked her voice.

"Tommy?"

He looked up. Shripton was standing there, rain dripping from his bowler hat, rain running down his black coat. His face was illuminated in flashes from the fireworks. He seemed sad.

"You can get up, Tommy."

Tommy looked around slowly. There were others there, but they didn't register. He was on the lower roof, a place of relative stability. His terror waned slightly. Carefully, steadily, he raised himself. He felt light. Frenna was no longer on his shoulders. A gust of wind made him crouch suddenly, but then he stood again, stooped like an old man.

"It's okay."

He saw Frenna. She was slumped over, supported over the shoulders of two blueshirts. She must have tried to escape, to make it somehow up the ladder herself, and been shot with an electric pistol. The others were nowhere to be seen. They had made it to the upper roof, and they must have run for it.

But there was nowhere for them to go.

Tommy took a step towards Shripton, and then collapsed onto him, weeping uncontrollably. "I couldn't do it!" he cried. "I couldn't do it! Oh, God, I couldn't do it! I'm sorry! I'm sorry! I'm so-o-o-oo-ry-y-y . . ." His voice drifted off, consumed by sobs that shook the two of them.

Shripton, engulfed by the bigger man, reached behind Tommy and patted him on the back. "I know," he whispered. "I know."

Then he lifted one of Tommy's arms from his shoulder, rolled up the sleeve, spread three of his fingers, and pressed the three marks on TeePee's left forearm.

*   *   *   *   *

Tommy Pierre Antikagamac slipped the shoulder pads over his head and onto his shoulders, where they fit like a part of his own body. He punched the chest plate with his two hands, a habitual gesture he did every time he put on pads. Around the world, a million young football players did the same thing.

The pre-game nerves were familiar, like an old friend who is back from a long trip. They were somewhat more intense than he remembered, and with good reason, this being his first game in almost two years. Had he lost anything? The question on his mind was the same one the sportswriters at *Luker* had asked and the same one that was on the lips of millions of football fans around the world.

But he felt fine. He liked the nervousness, the mental tension that preceded the physical contest on the field. It was all part of the game he loved. Nerves or not, everything was under control. He had the mental support, literally, of every player in this locker room.

Thousands upon thousands had eegressed to him their support. Win or lose, he was a hero. Just to be here, just to be getting back onto the field after being captured by Ketchen, brainwashed, after his struggle to rejoin the Hive – it was an accomplishment far more significant than beating the Paris Revolution would be. *But I hope you give those frogs from France the thumping of their lives!*

His indeed was a remarkable story. Over 8 million sports fans had ingressed his thoughts before the World Super Bowl, the last game he'd played. He knew that that number was going to be eclipsed today, even though it was only the season opener.

Of all the voices in his head, he picked out one in particular, and he smiled. *I hope you have many good interceptions today*, Frenna said.

Every time I throw an interception, I will think of you, he eegressed back. He felt her smile, and then felt her laugh when she realized from his thoughts that an interception was not a good thing. They hung on to that connection for a few moments before he let go to pursue more immediate matters.